WHITE JADE

Borgo Press Books by Victor J. Banis

*The Astral: Till the Day I Die * Avalon: An Historical Novel * The C.A.M.P. Cookbook * The C.A.M.P. Guide to Astrology * Charms, Spells, and Curses for the Millions * Color Him Gay: That Man from C.A.M.P. * The Curse of Bloodstone: A Gothic Novel of Terror * Darkwater: A Gothic Novel of Horror * The Daughters of Nightsong: An Historical Novel* (Nightsong Saga #2) * *The Devil's Dance: A Novel of Terror * Drag Thing; or, The Strange Tale of Jackle and Hyde * The Earth and All It Holds: An Historical Novel * A Family Affair: A Novel of Terror * Fatal Flowers: A Novel of Horror * Fire on the Moon: A Novel of Terror * The Gay Dogs: That Man from C.A.M.P. * The Gay Haunt * The Glass House: A Novel of Terror * The Glass Painting: A Gothic Tale of Horror * Goodbye, My Lover * The Greek Boy * The Green Rolling Hills: Writings from West Virginia* (editor) * *Green Willows: A Novel of Terror * Kenny's Back * Life & Other Passing Moments: A Collection of Short Writings * The Lion's Gate: A Novel of Terror * Love's Pawn: A Novel of Romance * Lucifer's Daughter: A Novel of Horror * Moon Garden: A Novel of Terror * Nightsong: An Historical Novel* (Nightsong Saga #1) * *The Pot Thickens: Recipes from Writers and Editors* (editor) * *San Antone: An Historical Novel * The Scent of Heather: A Novel of Terror * The Second House: A Novel of Terror * The Second Tijuana Bible Reader* (editor) * *The Sins of Nightsong: An Historical Novel* (Nightsong Saga #3) * *Spine Intact, Some Creases: Remembrances of a Paperback Writer * Stranger at the Door: A Novel of Suspense * Sweet Tormented Love: A Novel of Romance * The Sword and the Rose: An Historical Novel * This Splendid Earth: An Historical Novel * The Tijuana Bible Reader* (editor) * *Twisted Flames * The WATERCRESS File: That Man from C.A.M.P. * A Westward Love: An Historical Romance * White Jade: A Novel of Terror * The Why Not * The Wine of the Heart: A Novel of Romance * The Wolves of Craywood: A Novel of Terror*

WHITE JADE

A NOVEL OF TERROR

V. J. BANIS

THE BORGO PRESS

MMXII

FIRST BORGO PRESS EDITION

Published by Wildside Press LLC

www.wildsidebooks.com

I am deeply indebted to my friend, Heather, for all the help she has given me in getting these early works of mine reissued.

And I am grateful as well to Rob Reginald, for all his assistance and support.

CONTENTS

CHAPTER ONE

It was five full years since I had last seen Jeffrey Linton—five years since he had held me in his arms and kissed me while my heart pounded and my head went spinning.

I had not gone to his wedding. My broken heart was my own business. I was nineteen at the time and I thought I would die, that my heart could never mend and love would never come to me again.

Now I was twenty-four and if I had never fallen in love again, I could at least say with certainty that I was healed of that first love.

Still, it was a shock to find myself facing him once again, so without warning. Time, which is a sense experience after all and not a matter of so many measured intervals, disappeared in that first moment. All those years vanished. Christmas Channing was a nineteen year old again, her face flushing with delight.

"Chris," he said, in the soft sweet voice of old.

"Jeff." I moved instinctively toward him. He had changed very little. He would be twenty seven now, still slim and youthful, his dark hair spilling across his forehead as it always had, his lopsided grin giving my heart a tug.

"Jeff?" Another voice from deep inside the house. A woman's voice. Suddenly it brought those five years back to me, the intervening years. I glanced past him and stopped in my tracks.

"Forgive me," he said in a quick, low voice. "I played a trick on you to get you here because I need help badly, and you were the one person in the world I knew I could trust."

"I don't understand," I stammered. This was too sudden, too unexpected, for me to grasp.

He didn't let me finish. "I'll explain everything as soon as we're alone, I promise. But please, go along with whatever I say until then. It's urgent."

I pulled my hand from his with a jerk. A growing anger was taking the place of my initial surprise. I had traveled nearly two hundred miles from New York City for what appeared to be some shabby practical joke.

"I don't know why you brought me here under false pretenses," I said coldly, "but I don't think I want to stay."

"Chris." There was such an unmistakable note of urgency in his voice, such a look of pleading on his face, that it stopped me. "It means life and death to me. My life and death."

There was no time to argue the point or for further explanation. He had held me there too long for me to make an easy escape. Now there was a flurry of motion in the hall behind him and a woman appeared at his side.

I recognized her, although we had never met. At the time of her marriage to Jeffrey, she had appeared fairly often in the society columns. In that first painful year, especially in the weeks after their engagement was announced, I sought her name and picture almost daily, a self-inflicted torture. I had gotten over that, however, and in time ceased to read that section of the paper at all.

Mary Linton, née Morgan, was beautiful in an austere, chilling way. She held her head imperiously high and looked down upon us lesser mortals with haughty disdain. I could imagine the smile that would grace her elegant lips if she were told I was a druggist's daughter who had once been in love with her husband.

That was it, of course—that awful snobbishness and my childish reaction to it. I had suffered from that kind of snobbery all through the early years of school, the private school to which my father sent me, not because he could afford it but because my mother had died giving birth to me and he didn't have the time to look after me and run the store as well.

I had suffered that same disdain from a changing army of young women who sneered because I was a druggist's daughter who, they thought, aspired to their exalted station. It had made me distant in return. I had decided I wanted their friendship even less than they wanted mine. I remained independent and aloof ever after and, if I am to be completely honest, with a great big chip on my shoulder when it came to snobbish people.

That was what made me suddenly angry at her instead of him and put me, if only for a moment, on Jeffrey's side, without the faintest idea what Jeffrey's side was. I had loved him once with all the intensity of young love, and I resented her immediately not only because she had taken him from me (never a thought of his going) but because she was what she was, and that I had always resented. And without time to think about it, I was prepared to defend Jeffrey against her. It was silly but it was automatic, and it was settled before I could even think of its silliness.

"Hello," she said, looking me up and down as if I were a fish she was contemplating buying for dinner. "Who's this?"

"It's a Miss Channing." Jeff fixed his eyes on mine. "She's come about the job."

The cold look turned positively frigid. "She won't do," Mary Linton said.

"Good Lord, Mary, you haven't even spoken to her," Jeff said, fixing his eyes on mine. "How do you know she won't be just perfect?"

"No," I said sharply. I did not mean to be thrown back and forth between them, like a ping-pong ball in a tournament. "That's quite all right. I've decided the job isn't right for me." I turned to go.

"Wait," he said, and to my further humiliation, I did wait. "My wife is being very rude."

"Jeffrey...," she said.

"It's true. You are being rude. This young lady has come a long distance for an interview—"

"At whose suggestion?"

"Mine, blast it. I told you her letter sounded excellent and I wanted her to come up. And now here she is."

"Yes, here she is." His wife edged away from the anger in his voice and she yielded reluctantly. I did not delude myself however that this had in any manner increased her liking for me. "I must have forgotten you were coming. Come in, Miss... Banner, was it?"

"Channing," I said in my crispest voice. "Christmas Channing. My father called me that because I was born on Christmas day."

"How sweet." Her eyelashes flicked.

I hesitated as they stepped aside for me to come in. I did not want to enter this house. I did not want to be involved in whatever Jeffrey's problem was, or with Jeffrey Linton in any way.

My automatic resentment of his wife, however, had caused me foolishly to keep silent this long about my former relationship with Jeffrey. To admit to it now seemed to lend it an air of guilt. And to refuse to go in would seem childish after Jeffrey's defense of me.

Without seeming furtive or silly, there was nothing I could do but go past them into the house, holding my chin defiantly high in the way that Jeffrey used to tease me about. As the door swung shut, I promised myself I would make the interview brief, decline the job, and leave as quickly as I could.

"I'm afraid we've just lost a maid," Jeff said, "so we're sort of roughing it. Let me help you with your coat."

"It isn't necessary," I told him, "this won't take long, I'm sure."

"Don't be silly." He gave me one of those mocking grins that had once meant so much to me. "It's rather warm in here. I've been quite ill, you know."

I did not know but the words seemed weighted. And I did realize, looking into his face as he took my coat and gloves and scarf, that he had indeed been ill. I had been so shocked seeing him that I hadn't noticed how gaunt and deeply lined his face was, more than it should have been as a result of the five years. He was pale, strikingly so, his eyes had the dull, lightless look of the ill, and his mouth was drawn down.

I had a sudden feeling of malaise. I shivered even though it was warm in the hall.

"Of course she knows you've been ill," his wife said sharply, leading the way into a room off the hall. "Why else would you be interviewing a nurse to stay with us?"

Again my eyes met Jeffrey's. It was fortunate that his wife's back was turned to me. She could hardly have helped noticing my look of surprise. I knew nothing about nursing. I had come regarding a supposed secretarial job, to see a man who had given his name as Adams. I had come under no false pretenses, yet I suddenly found myself embroiled in a deception the purpose and extent of which I could not even guess. I was being placed in a position between a man I had once loved and his wife, who plainly did not like me.

"Come in, please," Jeffrey said.

He took my arm firmly, his grip so fierce that it was actually painful. The look he flashed me was so pathetic, so desperate, that I let him pilot me into the richly paneled sitting room into which his wife had preceded us.

It was a very handsome room, furnished in what I thought was the Queen Anne style, a room in which one should have felt immediately comfortable.

I felt as if I were stepping into a tomb.

CHAPTER TWO

Mary Linton crossed to a large writing table and ruffled impatiently through some papers there, leaving them in disarray.

"I'm afraid I don't find Miss Chandler's letter," she said without looking at her husband.

"Channing," I corrected her automatically.

Jeff frowned thoughtfully, then brightened. "I had it earlier, I was looking it over. I must have left it upstairs."

"Well, I should like to have it so I can judge Miss...uh... Manning's qualifications." She looked from him to me, I suppose expecting one of us to run for it. I had no intention of going, since I was not yet, and had no intention of being, in her employ. Apparently Jeff did not choose to go either.

After a moment she sighed grievously. "I suppose I'll have to get it." She left without excusing herself, looking increasingly annoyed.

When she had gone, I said rather quietly, "If she finds my letter, she will know I am not here about a nursing job."

"She won't find it." He smiled at me, a smile that blended gratitude and relief and something else I did not want to acknowledge, and came toward me with his arms outstretched.

I quickly sidestepped the intended embrace. Even if he were not married, and the circumstances of our reunion not so peculiar, I would not have wanted his arms about me.

He stopped short when I evaded him and although he continued to smile, his smile had a tinge of sadness now.

"So you've fallen out of love with me," he said.

"I have had plenty of time in which to do so." I was angry with him, angry with myself, angry with this silly situation in which I had somehow gotten involved. "And even if I hadn't, you could hardly expect me to welcome your embrace."

"You're still wearing the jade," he said, looking at my throat.

My hand automatically went to the pendant of white jade I wore. I had truly forgotten I was wearing it. I put it on each day without thinking about it, and no longer with the sense of anguish I had once felt. It was the gift he had given me when he asked me to marry him, in lieu of a ring.

"When you give jade," he explained, whispering in my ear, "you give a part of your soul with it. You will always wear my soul at your throat. I can never take it back."

"Your wife will be back in a moment," I said curtly. "If you have any idea of persuading me to continue this charade without telling her the truth, you have better explain to me why you brought me here under false pretenses."

He grew sober. "Because I'm in desperate need of help. You were the one person I felt sure I could trust."

"And why, after all these years, should you think of me? Why should you think you could trust me any more than anyone else?"

He looked down. "Maybe because I needed someone so desperately. And maybe because I hoped you might still love me."

"I think I had better go."

"No, please." He moved swiftly, seizing my arm again. "I hoped you would at least listen, for the sake of our past love."

I said nothing, but I did pause and wait for him to continue.

"I think my wife is planning to kill me," he said in a matter-of-fact voice, his eyes locked on mine. "I think, in fact, she has already begun."

"Kill you?" I was stunned. For a long moment I could only stare at him incredulously. Then, quite deliberately, I removed my arm from his grip and went to sit in one of the large wing chairs, trying to collect my wits.

"That's the most incredible thing I've ever heard. Why on earth should your wife want to kill you?"

"I know it's incredible. I didn't want to have to explain so abruptly, but you were going to leave. I had to stop you."

"You still haven't explained why she should want to kill you."

He glanced anxiously toward the hall but there was no sign of his wife. "Because I told her I don't love her. I told her I have never loved her."

I shook my head violently. "What nonsense," I said, as one would to a child. "This is the twentieth century, for Heaven's sake, and this isn't the house of the Borgias. People don't go around killing one another off because they aren't in love. There's divorce and—"

"Mary would never agree to a divorce. Use your head. Look at her. Is she the type of woman who would give up something that belongs to her?"

I didn't like being spoken to in that manner, but I held my tongue and allowed myself to think as he suggested. It was true, in a sense at least. Mary Linton and the scores of females like her I had known in school were not inclined to give up what they owned—and they would, to a woman, feel they owned a husband, particularly a suave, handsome one....

"This is ridiculous," I said, cutting off my own stream of thought and standing abruptly. "I can't imagine...your wife said you had been sick. Perhaps...."

He looked saddened and his smile went awry in a way that made me regret such a thought.

"You think I'm crazy," he said, more a statement of bitter fact than a question.

I shook my head frantically. "I don't know," I said, and meant it. "This is all so insane, the whole situation. I don't know what to think. I want to go. I think I should go, please."

A clock struck somewhere in the house. Nonsensically my thoughts went back into the past. There was a cuckoo clock in my father's house, an antiquated and not very accurate device with a gratingly loud cuckoo that announced the hour. It had struck as Jeff was proposing to me, so that he had to wait for it to finish before he could go on, and I had spoiled the romantic mood by giggling.

"Jeff," Mary Linton called from upstairs, "I can't find that blasted letter."

"It must be there." His eyes, trained on me while he answered her, were frightened as I had never seen them before. They imparted some of their fear to me. "Look in my desk."

"In the name of God," he spoke to me in a lowered voice, "do me one favor, Chris, that's all I ask, one favor."

I bit my lower lip. I had loved this man once. Even if I did not love him now—and I did not—did I not owe him one more favor at least, when he was so obviously sincere in his desperation?

He took my hesitant silence for assent. He went quickly to the writing table and took a cup and saucer from one corner of its top.

"My tea," he said. "She fixes it for me herself every day. A wifely gesture." He laughed but there was no humor in the bitter, harsh sound. I was struck again by how wasted he looked, how pale and drawn.

He opened a drawer and took a small jar from within, an ordinary jar that might have held applesauce of something equally innocent. It was empty. He removed the lid and poured the cup's contents into it, replacing the lid.

"Here." He brought the jar with its yellow brown contents across to me, "Take this to a chemist. Have it analyzed."

"But what on earth...?"

"I can't find it," Mary said from the stairs.

"Please," Jeff begged in a hoarse whisper.

I opened my purse—a generous carryall—and put the jar into it, clicking it shut as she came into the room.

"I can't find it anywhere," she said in a petulant tone. "It must have gotten lost."

"It's all right, darling." He gave her a smile so relaxed, so every day, that I thought I must have imagined all the other, the anxiety and fear and tension of the last few minutes. "Miss Channing isn't quite convinced she would want the job. I suppose she would prefer a younger patient, or a better-looking one."

"No," I said quickly, too quickly, and hurriedly added, "But it is a little far from New York."

"Surely you had the address to begin with," she said, further piqued at this answer. "Couldn't you have looked it up on a map?"

"I did." I knew that I sounded flustered. Pretense was not my forte. "I just didn't realize how far it was in actual distance until I got here. That long train ride...." I let the sentence trail off vaguely.

"Well, I suppose we ought to thank you for coming." She stepped aside for me to go. "Although I for one had no idea an appointment had even been made. My husband has been ill, as you know. He isn't thinking as clearly these days as he ought to be."

The thought came to me again that perhaps Jeff really wasn't in full control of his faculties. Perhaps it was wrong of me, even dangerous, to humor him as I was doing. It might be best, best even for him, if I told his wife everything now.

"Is something wrong?" she asked me.

"No," I managed to say, putting a protective hand across the front of my purse, where I could feel the bulk of the tea-filled jar. "I only thought that if I reconsider, I'll write you again and resend my qualifications."

"That will be fine." She was obviously confident this would never take place. She smiled more warmly than she had since I'd arrived. Apparently now that I was leaving she felt she could afford to be gracious to me.

"That's a handsome pendant you're wearing," she said. "White jade, isn't it?"

"Yes, thank you." I managed somehow to return her smile. I wondered if her smile would remain if she knew the jade had been a present from husband, an engagement present to me.

"It's rather like mine. That is, the jade is alike. Mine is in a ring."

She extended her hand for me to see the ring. It was a shock to see the stone, so like my own, mounted in gold. Jeff Linton had given away his soul rather freely, I thought. But I complimented her on it, making every effort to seem relaxed and natural.

I did not breathe easily until I was outside and the great door of the house was closed after me. Then, for the first time, I let my shoulders droop and the corners of my mouth turned down as they had wanted to do since I had first recognized Jeff.

It had started to snow. Delicate tufts of white danced and swirled, postponing their arrival on the ground as long as they dared.

It was afternoon. It would be evening by the time I reached the city, quite late by the time I had made it home and eaten dinner. I'd had lunch in the town of Elsinore, the nearest village, before coming up to the house for the interview.

The taxi that had brought me up from Elsinore, a twenty minute drive, was waiting as the driver had promised. He saw me come out the small gate and sat up sharply, twisting about on the seat to open the door for me without getting out of the car.

The seat in the rear was worn and shabby. Unfamiliar to me only a short time before, it now had a welcome air about it.

"Wasn't such a long talk," he said, starting off cautiously in the fresh snow, although very little remained more than a second or two on the ground. It was only October and still early for serious snow.

"No," I said thoughtfully. It seemed as if I had lived an entire lifetime since knocking at the door of that house and yet it had been only a matter of minutes, less than half an hour at most.

"Everything go well?" he asked in a friendly, not-prying way.

"It was...interesting."

"Going to be joining us?" he asked, as if the whole village were only an adjunct to the Linton household, as perhaps it was.

"I don't know," I answered. I turned to look through the rear window of the car. The house was vast and gray, made of weathered stone. Because it stood on a hill, it could be seen even from the town. I had watched it loom closer and closer on my way up. Then, it had seemed picturesque, with its turrets and mullioned windows. Now it looked ominous and foreboding. Through the gently falling snow its outlines were blurred, fading into the grayness of the sky. It might have been a ghost house, a mere illusion, a fragment from some childhood dream.

But it was real. And Jeff Linton was real. So was his fear. It had been like a living presence between us, that fear, making me agree to help him even against my better judgment, despite my conviction that his statements were ridiculous. People didn't just run about killing one another because they were a bit possessive.

But they did, of course. One did not read newspapers and watch television without knowing that people did murder one another, and sometimes for the slimmest of reasons.

In my purse, the bulk of the glass jar was like a haunting spirit reminding me of Jeff's anxiety.

I was afraid.

CHAPTER THREE

"Jeff, Jeff," I thought, "why couldn't you have stayed in the past?"

"I love you."

I had only to close my eyes, to lean back against the seat of the cab, and I could hear his voice speaking those words....

"I love you," he said. "Lord, how I've missed you. I couldn't begin to tell you."

"Try." It seemed to me as if he had been gone months instead of weeks.

"You haven't said you love me," he said with a mock pout. He looked down and saw the jade pendant at my throat. "I'll bet you haven't worn that since I left."

"Silly, of course I have. I haven't had it off once. And I do love you. I love you for always and always."

We kissed, a long, searching kiss. Jeff, my darling Jeff. I could still scarcely believe we were going to be married, that anyone so handsome and worldly as Jeff could be interested in spending his life with me.

But he was, and I had the white jade to remind me. Not that I was likely to forget.

"You didn't say always," I teased him.

"Always is an awfully long time, darling. Can't we settle for now?"

"Oh, no, you don't get off that easily." I got up from the sofa and went to the battered upright piano, running my fingers over the keys. A melody came to mind and my fingers picked it out instinctively.

He came to stand behind me, his hands at my waist. "Pretty," he said.

"Grieg." I hit a sour note and stopped. All the girls at school learned to play and my father, thinking that synonymous with talent, had insisted on a piano here, but neither learning to read music nor learning to love it could have made a pianist out of me.

"I may not have meant the music," he said.

I leaned back against him and sighed contentedly.

"What if it weren't?" he asked.

"If what weren't?"

"If it weren't forever?"

I had a quick moment of panic. Oh, lord, no, don't let it end. Don't let me lose him, ever.

I laughed and rapped another key. "I suppose you're going to tell me you met some fabulous heiress in Florida and you've decided I'm not up to snuff after all—a mere druggist's daughter."

He kissed the back of my neck. I suddenly felt edgy.

"Well?" I asked after a long silence.

"Well, what?"

"Did you meet a lot of wealthy heiresses who turned your head?" I looked over my shoulder at him. I was smiling, but there was something ominous about the mood, the tone of the conversation.

He said, still smiling, "Only one." He lit a cigarette and went to sit in Dad's old chair.

"Was she awfully pretty?"

"In her own way." He gave me the impression he was playing cat and mouse with me, which only upset me the more.

"What exactly does that mean?"

"She's the cold, austere type. Plenty of breeding, lots of money and class and elegance. Quite beautiful, really, but not cute and pert like you."

"You know, all my life I've thought it would be nice if I were one of the beautiful ones and some of them were cute and pert."

He laughed and puffed on his cigarette. "You've nothing to be jealous of, little one."

"Who was she?"

"Who? Oh, the heiress. Mary Morgan. New York family, in glass. You've probably heard of it—Morgan Glassware."

"And I suppose you thought of marrying her for her money," I said with a giggle.

"Yes, I did," and he laughed too.

* * * * * * *

It was about a month after that when I learned the truth. Until then, except for that conversation with its worrisome overtones, I had not even a clue that anything was amiss. Jeff had seen a little less of me, it was true, but that had been credited to some new responsibilities at his job.

It wasn't an awfully good job, with an advertising firm. He wanted to be an actor, but the parts had been few and far between. We had talked it over and agreed that the advertising firm had possibilities, and if he worked hard there might be some future in it. So I could hardly complain if he devoted a lot of his evenings and even some of his weekends to work.

My father had never been very good at keeping things from me, so I knew when I came in on that particular evening that something was odd. He was much too solicitous.

"Snappy out there," he said, jumping up from his chair to give me a hand with my coat, for which I gave him a curious look. "Better sit down and get warm. Why don't you let me fix you some tea?"

"No, don't fuss, please." I gave his shoulder an affectionate pat. He had only gotten out of bed a week before, after a particularly bad spell. "I'll get it myself. You sit and relax, all right?"

I thought I would wait and see if he brought up whatever it was that he had on his mind. If not, I would broach it for him. It came up sooner than I had expected, however.

"Where's the newspaper?" I asked, coming back into the living room a few minutes later with my tea.

"The paper?" he looked so confused by that question that I knew something was definitely wrong. "It doesn't seem to be here, does it? Could I have thrown it out with the trash? Let me think...."

"Dad it's no use," I said, smiling. "You may as well come clean and tell me whatever it is you're trying to hide. You know I'll get it out of you anyway."

He looked sheepish. "Chris," he said, and then couldn't bring himself to say whatever it was. He got up and went into his room, and came back a moment later with the evening paper.

Until now I had been mostly amused, but as he handed me the paper, I had a presentiment of what I was going to learn. The paper was open to the society page. How on earth he had even come across the announcement I couldn't guess, since he was not given to reading the society columns. Something must have caught his eye as he turned through the section.

I truly had not given any thought to Jeff's beautiful heiress since that one conversation, but I recognized the name at once" "Mary Morgan to Wed," the headline announced. I suppose I knew without reading further who the bridegroom was going to be. I was less surprised than I would have expected to be.

I never saw him again until that unsettling meeting in Elsinore. At first, because I was young and in love and thought the world ought to accommodate itself to that fact, I refused to accept it as the truth. I waited, thinking he would call and assure me it had been some awful silly mistake.

He didn't call, and I went through another stage in which I railed and swore how much I hated him, and avoided the truth in my father's eyes. I would never speak to him again, I vowed. He could come back, begging for forgiveness, and I would spit on him.

In the end, hating myself for the humiliation I was subjecting myself to, I went to him. Or at least I tried to. I went to his apartment. I rang the bell and listened, positive I heard him inside.

I knocked and I cried and I called his name until the blowsy woman who lived next door came out to investigate the ruckus.

If he was there, inside, he never opened the door, any more than he answered the phone, or replied to my letters, letters that were increasingly desperate, increasingly shameless.

I don't know what cruel sense of humor, what perverse emotion, brought him to send me an invitation to his wedding. I often wondered afterward how he explained my name on the list. Even more heartbreaking, I wondered how he had intended to introduce me to his bride if I had been so bold as to show up.

But of course I did not. He had known I would never come. He had always known, better than I, just what I would do.

CHAPTER FOUR

It was evening when I came through the vaulted waiting room at Grand Central and out into the cold air again. There was no snow falling here. It was a chilly autumn evening. The raucous after-work traffic had begun to thin.

Ordinarily I would take the subway home, but I was tired from the long trip and from the strain of anxiety. I got into a cab and gave the driver the address of my little apartment in the village.

The city that should have been familiar to me appeared jangled and strangely alien. I had a sense of disassociation that I could neither understand nor set aside. I leaned forward and said to the driver, "Take 42nd over to Eighth and down Eighth."

It was a slower route but there was no reason why he should mind. We inched our way through Times Square and then we were moving along Eighth Avenue.

"Wait, stop here for a moment," I said. He gave me a dubious look in the mirror but he pulled over to the curb.

The drugstore was still a drugstore, its brick front recently whitewashed. I did not remember clearly the man who had bought it. He had been soft spoken and placid of expression. I had only a vague image of white hair and spotted hands.

I could remember all of the store, however, with the worn, thin flooring and the old cabinets, some of them dating back before my birth. The big old fans at the ceiling spun lazily during the summer, little more than rippling the warm air.

The soda fountain with its black marble top and dilapidated

fixtures had always been crowded in the hour or so after school let out. The pharmacy counter, with its apothecary jars of colored water had so fascinated me as a child.

Behind the prescription counter stairs went up to our apartment above, small and ordinary, but comfortable. A little balcony opened off the living room. I could look up from the taxi window and see the railing still. I had kept potted geraniums on it. It was here that Jeff had proposed to me, standing in the blending light of moon and neon. He had slipped the white jade about my neck and told me he loved me.

No geraniums graced the balcony now. A wet rug hung over the wrought iron to dry.

"Drive on," I said, leaning back against the seat again.

How had I come to have the past so suddenly thrust upon me again? I had worked hard to rid myself of it—moving into a place of my own, breaking all the old ties, losing myself first in school and then in work.

At first it had seemed hopeless, as if I would never be relieved of that weight of unhappiness, losing first Jeff and then my father so soon after. Gradually, however, the wounds healed, as they must. I had begun to feel like and less like misery's child and more and more my own servant.

I had rediscovered the great joy to be found in little things— the laughter of a child, the scent of a rose, the sound of distant singing as someone passed beneath my window. I had learned to laugh, and to laugh at myself, and even to sing as I passed under windows.

One day I had awakened to discover to my surprise that I was happy, that I loved life, that I was one with the world again. The past was dead and buried—or so I had thought.

Now that dead past had risen from the grave to haunt me. I would have liked to turn my back on it, ignore it, let it die again, but in my purse I felt the weight of that jar I carried. It might have been all the tea ever brewed, it weighed so heavily.

* * * * * * *

In the morning I took the bottle to have the tea analyzed. I did not go to the shop that had been my father's, although of course that kindly old man who had it now could have done what I needed.

That was another of the ties from the past that I had severed, and when I had need of a pharmacy I went to a little one near my apartment where the pharmacist, only a year or two out of school, flirted a bit half-heartedly. This shop was all chrome and glass and sparkle. It had no soda fountain. It had no romance, but at least it inspired a certain confidence.

"Hello," Jerry, the young pharmacist, greeted me when I came in. "How'd the job interview go?"

"Still undecided." I gave him a wan smile. I had slept poorly.

I took my ominous burden from my purse and set it atop the counter. "I want to have this analyzed," I said. "Can you take care of that sort of thing for me?"

He picked up the jar and looked at it. "What's in it?"

"That is why I want to have it analyzed."

He unscrewed the lid and sniffed. "Smells like tea." At my impatient sigh, he said, quickly, "Okay, okay, it's not really up my alley, you understand, but I know a man.... Got any ideas yourself what to look for?"

I hesitated for a moment before shaking my head. It was no use making guesses. For all I knew—and I hoped it would be so—it was nothing but tea with a dash of lemon and maybe some sugar.

"Fine, be mysterious," he said, grinning as he replaced the lid. "I'll give you a call when I find out, unless you're in some sort of hurry."

"I am, a little, actually." I might be, or I might not, depending entirely upon what he found in that brownish liquid, but there was no use trying to explain that.

He gave a mock grimace and a shrug of resignation. "I'll see if I can find out anything today. That suit you better?"

I managed a grateful smile. "Yes." Then, growing sober, I added, "There is one more thing. I don't know how this works, but if you could exercise a little discretion...."

"Sure," he said, too quickly. I saw the guarded look that came into his eyes and I knew this was becoming a bit suspicious looking. Why should I want to have something whose properties were completely unknown to me analyzed so quickly and so quietly? I searched my mind for some excuse.

"Someone recommended it to me as a home remedy." That story sounded lame even to my own ears. "I thought better safe than sorry."

He looked unconvinced but for the moment he accepted my story.

"How about dinner somewhere tonight?" I asked with false brightness.

Which successfully changed the subject. His easy grin returned. "Sure. How about Mamma's? At eight?"

"Fine. I'll meet you there." A customer waited behind me and I could step aside with a last friendly smile and a nod, and make my escape while he temporarily forgot my mysterious bottle.

I had only to endure a day of anxious waiting and wondering, trying to convince myself that the passing minutes were not grating upon my nerves as if they were hours.

He was already there when I arrived at the restaurant. He looked happy and unconcerned and I tried to match my mood to his. I did not want to seem too anxious by asking what, if anything, he had learned and since he did not volunteer any information, I vowed to spend a quiet, pleasant evening in his company as if there was nothing of importance on my mind.

Mamma herself greeted us as we left the bar for the dining room, her shy, sweet smile making us welcome at once and dispelling the chill from the cold winds outside.

"Winter is here, no," she said, leading us to one of the romantic little nooks in the rear.

'It's close," Jerry said. I found myself thinking of Elsinore, where yesterday it had been snowing. "What'll it be?" he asked me when we were seated.

"You order for me." I didn't say that I could not concentrate my attention long enough to decide on food.

For all of that, though, the food did help. I took strength from the Barolo wine he ordered and I ate with gusto the steaming soup, tender leaves of spinach simmered in a rich chicken broth.

"The secret of good pasta," Jerry said when that was being served, "is the right degree of doneness. I had a friend who tested it by throwing strands against the wall. It was his theory that when the pasta was at just the right state, it would stick to the wall."

"And did it?" I asked, amused. Jerry fancied himself something of a food expert. At least he managed to make meals more interesting with his stories.

"Never did when I was around. We threw a lot of spaghetti at the wall one night and ended up with very little to eat. He thought maybe something was wrong with the plaster."

We were having tagliatelle, the pale, noodle-like pasta. "According to legend," he said, adding a dash of grated cheese, "this was inspired by the flaxen hair of none other than Lucrezia Borgia."

"I hope the color of her hair was her only contribution. Wasn't she the one so notorious for poisoning...?" I stopped midsentence, a sudden, awful image of Mary Linton popping into my mind. She too had pale yellow hair, so in contrast to my dark-haired plainness.

Our eyes met across the table. It was no good pretending. I put my fork down and drank a little of my wine.

"You'd better tell me," I said.

"I spent an hour or so this afternoon fielding some rather peculiar questions," he said, looking down at his plate and twirling a fork idly in the tagliatelle. "Tell me something, just what was this friend of yours trying to cure with this little brew?"

I was too impatient to play games. "What was in it, Jerry?"

"Oh, a little tea, a little lemon, a little arsenic...."

I caught my breath sharply and said, too loudly, "Arsenic?"

He motioned me to lower my voice and glanced around, but no one seemed to have noticed my startled exclamation.

"Was there...very much arsenic?" It sounded, even as I asked it, a particularly foolish question. What did it matter just exactly how much arsenic there was in a cup of tea, when there oughtn't to be any there at all?

"Do you want it in scientific terms?"

"No, no, just...how dangerous would it be?"

He was silent for a moment, still toying with his pasta. The scent of food drifted upward from my neglected dinner. A few minutes before it had been a delicious aroma. Now it sickened me.

"Any arsenic is dangerous," he said finally. "There wasn't enough in that tea to kill anybody...."

I breathed a sigh of relief—prematurely as it turned out.

"Not with just that one dose, at least."

It took a minute for the implication to become clear. "Can arsenic be given over a period of time?" I asked hesitantly. "I mean, if it were given that way, would it eventually prove fatal, even though the individual doses were small?"

"Is it cumulative, you mean? Yes. This dosage is quite small, as a matter of fact. A strong, healthy person wouldn't really suffer much ill effect from it. A bit of queasiness, some fatigue. He'd probably think of himself as a bit 'out of it,' and go about his business as usual."

"But if he took repeated doses?"

"If he took several like this over a period of say a few weeks, he would gradually become sick. So long as he kept taking this tea, assuming it had the same surprising ingredient in it, he would just keep getting sicker and sicker without knowing why. It's the kind of symptom that is vague enough, he might not even get around to seeing a doctor, particularly with all the mysterious viruses and touches of something going around today."

"What symptoms would he have, exactly?" I was seeing Jeff's pale, drawn face, thinner than it ought to have been.

"Headaches, nausea, maybe vomiting as it went along, some muscular cramps, a general debilitation—all getting progressively worse."

"Until...?"

"Until he died." He paused. "Of course, I'm not expert on poisons. I could refer you to a toxicologist, if you like."

I shook my head. "No, that won't be necessary." It didn't matter greatly if some of the fine points of what he told me were inaccurate. The important thing was that the poison was there, in the tea, and that it could make someone sick, and eventually kill them.

"Chris, look." He reached across the table to take my hand. "Is there something you want to talk about? Are you in any kind of spot? Because if someone really gave you this stuff as a remedy, something is rotten in Denmark."

In Denmark? I was thinking, in Elsinore. And hadn't that been the name of Hamlet's castle? Yes, something was very rotten in Denmark.

Aloud, I said, "No, it isn't anything, really. I know it all sounds very mysterious and dramatic, but it's only one of those mistakes that occur."

I gave him a forced smile. He did not believe me, of course.

"Okay." He let go of my hand. "Only remember, I'm close by if you need me."

But you won't be close by, I thought later, staring across my living room at a cheap brown and blue copy of the Picasso woman, *you'll be here and I will be in Elsinore. If I go.*

And there was the rub. Need I go at all?

It might, after all, be nothing more than some bizarre mistake. What did people use arsenic for, anyway? Rat poison? Or some sort of cleaning job? Might it not have gotten accidentally onto the tea leaves, soaked in, so that a truly innocent and devoted act on the part of Mary Linton was causing her husband to be poisoned?

Then I had only to write to Jeff and tell him what I had learned. He could discover for himself if the tea leaves were accidentally soaked with arsenic (was arsenic liquid, I wondered. And if powder, wouldn't it be noticed on the leaves when the tea was brewed.)

Of even if his fears were true, if Mary was trying to murder him, then my letter would confirm the fact. He had only to leave.

Except, he had looked really awful that day—was it only two days ago? And how did a man as sick as he obviously was justify wanting to go out for a stroll in winter snow.

I went impatiently into the kitchen to pour myself a cup of coffee. Usually at this time of evening I drank tea, but I had tried that earlier and found it unpalatable.

All right, look at in the worst possible light, I told myself. Suppose Mary Linton was trying to murder Jeff. Suppose he were already sick enough that he could do nothing about it, couldn't escape, had no one to whom he could turn for help (he had said that, hadn't he?)

So what did that have to do with me? I wasn't in love with him. He wasn't, I was quite sure, in love with me. We had not seen one another for five years and at that time, when I had been in love, he had jilted me. Coldly, cruelly, not caring at all if I nearly died from heartache. I owed him nothing.

Which of course was utter nonsense. Nearly dying from heartache was a far cry from literally dying from arsenic poisoning.

And I did owe him, in the same sense that Jerry owed me some concern and his friend owed Jerry some concern, and so on and on through the whole structure that man had built up for himself and called civilization.

Because we are, in some measure at least, our brother's keepers. Because there are the dues we have to pay as part of the entire scheme, part of the human race. Because it is necessary to balance the ledger sheet against all the acts of concern and kindness that other people had done to me and would do again.

I went into my tiny bedroom, to my closet. The little overnight case was on the shelf. I took it down, carrying it to the bed. It had a film of dust on it and I got a cloth from the kitchen and dusted it carefully. Then I opened it and began to put things into it.

There was a train shortly after midnight that, with connections, would put me into Elsinore about dawn.

I could not help wondering what time of day Jeff usually had his tea.

CHAPTER FIVE

It was barely dawn when I arrived at the little station in Elsinore. I felt old and haggard in the first timid light of morning.

Now that I was here, standing outside the station on the empty street, I felt a trifle foolish as well. Last night, spurred on by fear and tension, it had seemed imperative that I get here as soon as possible.

It would have made a great deal more sense to have waited for the morning train. There was nothing I could do at this hour. It was quite unlikely that anyone, including Jeff, would be stirring in that big stone house. I had rushed here so that I could kill time waiting for a propitious hour to go there.

I left my overnight case at the station, after first using its contents to freshen my appearance a little. The station's coffee shop was not yet open but the old man working there sent me to another just a few blocks down the street that was doing business.

I came into its brightly lit warmth gratefully. A few local men were already having coffee on their way to work. The waitress, a plump, jolly looking creature, eyed me with frank curiosity.

"Bit nippy out, isn't it?" she said in the way of a greeting.

"Yes. I'll have coffee, black, please, and one of those doughnuts."

She brought the coffee in a big, battered looking mug and then fetched the doughnut. "You're not from Elsinore, are you?" she asked in a friendly voice.

I did not want a get-acquainted chat, however, nor did I want to explain who I was or why I was here. "No, I'm not," I said, softening it a little with a smile. I took my coffee and doughnut to one of the tables near the window and pretended to study the scene outside.

An hour and several cups of coffee later, I left and walked back to the station, where I guessed rightly that I would find a taxi. I hadn't expected to find the same man who had driven me before, but there he was, smiling broadly in recognition.

"Morning, Miss," he greeted me, "looks like you'll be taking the job up at the house after all. I guess you'll want a lift?"

"Yes," I said, letting him help me into the back seat of his aged vehicle. I did not try to make any explanations for my return.

When we were close to the house, however, I leaned forward and asked him to pull over and stop. "I'd like to walk the rest of the way," I said. "It's so pretty out here, away from the city."

"We don't have a lot to offer, but it is pretty," he agreed, making change. "Especially with the house up there above everything, looking so majestic, if you know what I mean."

I got out and then, remembering something, leaned back in. "I want to try to catch Mrs. Linton," I said. "Do you happen to know sort of car she has?"

"One of those big foreign jobs. A Rolls Royce, they call it. But you needn't worry about that, she's not likely to be going out this early. Will you be wanting me to come back for you, Miss, or will you be staying this time?"

How could I answer that? I hardly knew myself when I would be going. As soon as possible, of course, but I couldn't say that to him.

"Thank you, I'll call if I need a ride back." I closed the door with a last nod.

I waited until he had made his turn and started back for town. Then I set out toward the house. I did not follow the road but cut across the fields. The snow that had fallen when I was last here had disappeared. The ground was bare and dead looking, and easy to walk on.

As I walked, I stared at the house before me. It did not look pretty to me, or majestic. It appeared dark and brooding, as if it watched me with countless, malevolent eyes, letting me come closer, closer, until it could reach out....

Stop it, I told myself sharply. There were dangers here that were real enough without letting my imagination run away with me as well.

I did not go directly to the house. Between me and it were several trees in a cluster, bare now, their branches making a twisted pattern. My coat was dark and long, in a pattern of browns and tan and black—the barren earth colors. In it I thought I would blend all right with the trees and the winter scene. I took up a post between two of the larger trees and began to wait.

The cabbie's remark indicated that I might have a long wait, but there was nothing I could do for it. If it proved more than I could bear, I would simply have to return to town and try again later. At some time Mary Linton would be going out. That was when I would go to see Jeff.

I had no watch and could only guess at the passage of time. It seemed to stretch on and on forever. I had worn my warmest clothes but even so I eventually had to stamp my feet and rub my hands together to ward off the cold that was seeping into my very bones.

The distant house remained still. Once a maid in black uniform came out and went to the garages behind the main building and returned a few minutes later. I had no way of knowing whether the master and mistress were still in bed or up or, for all I really knew, on vacation in Florida.

Just as I had decided I could bear the cold no longer, fortune smiled on me. I saw a man open one of the garage doors and a minute later a mammoth looking Rolls Royce backed out and came around the drive to the front of the house. The driver went into the house, leaving the car running.

A few minutes later a woman came out. At the distance I could see little more than that it was a woman in a leopard coat, but she walked with an imperious carriage. I was sure it was she.

She got into the car and a moment later it moved off down the driveway and along the road toward town. I waited until she was out of sight before I moved from the protective cover of the trees.

I arrived at the house without incident except that I felt half dead from the cold. My numb fingers had some trouble with the big brass knocker.

The young woman in a maid's uniform who answered the door looked at me with some curiosity. I saw her eyes go past me to the drive, where no vehicle awaited me, and no doubt I looked frozen solid. I certainly felt it.

"I'd like to see Mr. Linton," I said.

"I've afraid he's not able to see visitors," she said in an apologetic voice.

My heart skipped a beat. "Is he very ill?"

"Yes, he's been in bed since yesterday. The flu."

I did not think his difficulty was the flu but I did not tell her this. "Please, it's important," I said instead. "Would you at least tell him I'm here? Tell him it's Miss Channing."

"Yes, Miss, I'll tell him." She hesitated. "You look awfully cold. Would you like to wait in here, it's warmer?" She indicated the Queen Anne sitting room.

I thanked her. She left me and I went in there, taking off my gloves and scarf and savoring the room's warmth.

She was back in just a few minutes. "Mr. Linton will see you," she said, studying me with fresh interest. "If you'll come with me, please."

I was shocked to see how dreadful he looked. Even the dimness of the room, with its draperies closed against the day's light, could not conceal the fact that he had deteriorated in the short time since I had seen him last.

"Jeff," I said, starting toward the bed in which he lay, propped up with pillows.

He gave me a warning glance and said past me, "That will be

all, thank you, Susan."

I waited until the door had closed after her before I came to the bed, instinctively putting a hand to his forehead. It felt cold and damp.

Our eyes met, his seeking in mine the answers that I did not want to give to the questions he did not want to ask.

"I was right, wasn't I?" he asked after a moment. His voice was an old man's voice, cracked and thin.

I nodded. "There was arsenic in the tea. Oh, Jeff, we've got to get away from here while Mary is out. We can—"

He gave his head a weary shake. "Impossible. I can barely manage to sit up."

He was right, of course, I realized that at once. Even if he were able to get out of the bed and into his clothes, how was I to get him from the house, into town, to New York City? A wave of frustration and despair swept over me, chilling me even more than the cold air in which I had waited earlier.

"What are we going to do?" I hadn't thought beyond telling him of the arsenic and helping him to leave.

His head had fallen weakly to one side. Now, with an apparent effort, he lifted it to look searchingly into my face again.

"Chris," he said in a whisper, "you must take the job as my nurse."

"But...but I can't," I stammered. "I know nothing about nursing."

"That doesn't matter. I'm not sick, except for the poison. If you can protect me from that, for a few days even...." His voice trailed off, as if even the effort of speaking was too much.

"Couldn't I...couldn't I just go into town and find someone to help? The local sheriff...yes, that's...."

He gave his head a violent shake. "No. Don't you think I've thought of all that? Don't you think I'd have taken this whole thing to him before if I thought there was any chance he'd listen?"

"But he must listen...."

"Listen to what? A lot of unfounded accusations? I have no

evidence."

"The tea."

"That's not here now, is it? There's only your word for it that it was poisoned, or that I gave it to you. Do you think they'll believe you when they find out who you are and what we once were to one another? You're forgetting, this is Mary's town. She and her family have virtually owned it for generations. You and I are outsiders."

I knew that what he said was true. Even the taxi driver had spoken with affectionate awe of the house. And if we made any sort of charges, we would have to tell the whole truth about our past relationship. I could easily imagine how that would make everything look.

I took a deep breath, willing myself calm. "What can we do?"

"Go back to New York." He spoke as if he had already gone over all this countless times in his mind. "Write a letter, giving a lot of qualifications for the job, and say you've decided you'll take it."

"I haven't any qualifications."

"Make them up. I'll take care of checking them."

"What if your wife won't have me? She wasn't exactly enthusiastic about me before."

"You'll get the job, don't worry." He gave me a wan smile. I was forgetting, of course, Jeff had always managed to get whatever he wanted, particularly from a woman. "But time is precious. Write at once, please, and be ready to come immediately."

Still I hesitated. It was so beyond anything I had experienced before. I was no hero and certainly no actress. There wasn't the slightest possibility of my carrying it off.

He saw my indecision and when he spoke again it was with a note of urgent pleading in his voice. "Mary only went on a brief errand. She'll be back in a few minutes, Chris."

I met his anxious eyes. He reached out with effort and took my hand. His felt frail and nearly lifeless.

"All right," I said in a small voice. "I had better go."

"I'll never forget this," he said.

The maid had disappeared and the halls were empty I ran down the stairs as if pursued by demons, as if the very house itself threatened me.

I reached the front door, fairly bursting through it—and ran into the arms of a man.

CHAPTER SIX

"What the...?" he exclaimed, as startled as I was by the collision.

I caught only a glimpse of him, before I thought to lower my face so he would not get a good look at me. He was tall and hatless. His hair was dark. He wore only a corduroy jacket and beneath it his shoulders were broad and square.

"I'm sorry," I stammered. "I should have gone the back way."

"Who are you?" he demanded in a voice that said quite plainly he was used to exercising authority.

"No one," I said, and in the next breath, "I came about a job."

I didn't give him time to question me further. Stepping quickly around him I ran down the steps and then slowed to a fast walk, not wanting to seem as if I were fleeing the place.

After a moment, I glanced back. He was still at the top of the steps, staring after me. I thought he had a faint smile on his lips, but as I looked, he turned and went inside. I thought, he's too tall, he'll hit his head, but he went in without a bump and without bowing or relinquishing any of his arrogance.

In a twinkling I knew who he was, the knowledge coming from forgotten bits of information I had long since stored in my subconscious. Mary Morgan Linton had a brother, his name was—I frowned—David.

This must be David. Certainly he was no servant. He had too commanding a manner. He had not even apologized for our accident, although of course it was I who ran into him.

Would he remember me? I thought not. He could not have

had more than a glimpse of me, and he thought I was merely someone seeking employment. Why should he attach any importance to me?

Mostly likely, I would never see him again anyway. He did not live there, I was sure of that. And when I came back, I would soon be gone once more, so I was not likely to meet him again.

I put him from my mind and starting walking. I had a long hike into town. I thought of my friendly taxi driver but there was no way of summoning him. Maybe, I thought wishfully, he'll just appear. He might have some reason to come out this way, and drive by and see me. Maybe....

He did not, however, happen to drive by. I saw him four days later when, for the third time in a week, I got off the train at Elsinore.

"Well, well," he greeted me when I approached the taxi stand, "becoming a regular visitor, looks to me."

"This time I'm planning to stay a while." I smiled at him, grateful to see a familiar face, however limited our acquaintance. I expected no friendly welcomes when I reached the Linton home.

For all that I knew, I might be too late. Perhaps Jeff was already...but I would not let myself think the rest of that. He knew I was coming. My letter, sent special delivery as soon as I returned to the city, had been answered with equal speed. In businesslike language, as if we did not know one another beyond that one, brief meeting, it accepted me for the position and suggested that I come at the first opportunity.

The driver brought me up to Morgan House—as he informed me the townspeople knew it—and after helping me with my bags and bidding me well, left. Once again I approached that massive door and lifted the heavy brass knocker. I thought of the little maid who had admitted me the last time. Would she remember me and comment on that visit?

It was not she who answered the door, however. It swung open and I found myself looking up into a handsome face— finely chiseled nose, lips set in a hard line above a square chin, eyes dark and piercing. I had seen that face before, had looked up into it quite recently when I collided with him in this same doorway. David Morgan, Mary's brother.

For a moment we stood as if suspended in time. I had seconds in which to realize how handsome he was. He wore riding clothes that well became him. The fitted breeches, the gleaming boots, the beautifully cut coat that revealed the width of his shoulders, all accentuated an aura of masculinity and strength.

The moment ended, the spell broke.

"Hello," he said, his tone neither welcoming me nor rejecting me.

"I'm Miss Channing." Something in his gaze made me feel suddenly embarrassed and I looked down, annoyed that his arrogant maleness should intimidate me in this way. "I've been employed to look after Mr. Linton."

"Yes. Come in." He stepped aside for me. I went past him, into the big central hall. "We just lost a maid. I'll see if I can find the housekeeper." He started away and paused, studying me intently. "Have we met before?"

I had been waiting for this and had my answer ready. "I was here once before for an interview. I believe we met then."

Recognition came into his eyes. "Oh, yes, the young lady who runs people down."

"I believe I apologized at the time," I said, angry and turning red. He was no less arrogant and rude than his sister and I felt no less resentful toward him.

"I'll see if I can find Mrs. Evans," he said, dismissing that other subject as of no importance. No doubt he viewed me the same way. Without waiting for a reply he strode down the hall, his step firm and purposeful, the walk of a man who always knew exactly where he was going—and always got there.

I turned over the new information he had given me. The maid who'd met me before was gone. Jeff had foreseen that danger and somehow gotten rid of her. I felt sorry for her, of course, but under the circumstances he'd had little choice. I hoped he had been generous.

I frowned, remembering. David Morgan had said, "We just lost a maid...." Which suggested that he was staying here in the house. I couldn't think offhand just how this would complicate things, if at all. It might even be an advantage to have a strong-minded man about. I'd have to think about that for a while.

I felt that my admitting to our previous meeting was a safe enough ploy, however. I had only seen him on the one visit, and I had seen Mary on one visit. There was no reason at all to suppose they would compare dates and discover that those meetings did not occur at the same time. But I made a mental note to tell Jeff, just in case.

I reflected ruefully that I really was ill-suited to intrigue.

Mrs. Evans, as it turned out, was a small, birdlike creature who moved with little fluttery gestures, as if not quite prepared to light in any one spot.

"Things have been so topsy-turvy," she said, leading me up the stairs, "the help coming and going so fast you can't even get a girl trained, and Mr. Linton being so sick. That's his room, there." She pointed at the door to his room. "I've put you right next to it, where it'll be convenient for you to come and go."

She ushered me into a small, pleasantly furnished room. It had a fireplace, before which were two comfortable looking chairs covered in chintz, with a footstool and a little lamp-topped table. The bed was an old fourposter covered with a thick comforter. The room was less elegant than the rest of the house, but with more charm.

"I hope this will be all right," she said. "It isn't the best room in the house."

"I think it's lovely." She seemed a bit at a loss as to how she should treat me. A private nurse was somewhat removed from ordinary house servants, in a station above, say, a maid, and yet hardly the same as a house guest. I thought it best to put her at ease and if possible make friends with her. I would certainly need friends in this house. "I'm not much for things too grand."

"I know just what you mean," she said, seeming pleased. "It makes my back a little stiff if you know what I mean. Give me a bit of chintz and a nice fireplace. Not that I'm not happy here, you understand," she added quickly. "And I hope you will be, too."

"I'm sure I shall." The fire had been laid but not lit. From the window I had a view toward the rear of the property. I could see the garages and the stables. David Morgan's costume had told me there must be horses and I wondered if I might be permitted to ride. Although I was city bred, riding lessons had been part of the standard curriculum for finishing-school girls and I considered myself a competent horsewoman.

Beyond the estate buildings stretched open fields and gently rolling hills and in the distance, but not particularly far away, thick, sprawling woods. It would be good riding country, a real pleasure after years of riding in Central Park.

"If there's anything you want, or you've got any questions, you just ring that little bell there." She indicated a button on the wall near the door. "I hope you'll be comfortable."

"And I hope we will be good friends."

"Oh, I'm sure we will be, Miss," she said, almost twittering.

When she had gone I stood for a moment more looking about the room. What nonsense, to stand and contemplate the pleasure of a ride through the woods, as if I were on holiday, as if a man's life wasn't hanging in the balance.

I put myself grimly to unpacking my things. My life might be in danger as well. I must keep that fact in mind, never forgetting for a moment. I had come for one reason alone—murder was being done in this house. And, if one, why not two?

CHAPTER SEVEN

A real nurse, I supposed, would know the routine that ought to be followed, but I was in ignorance. Should I go directly to Jeff's bedroom, careful to remember that he was Mr. Linton, whom I had met just once before, for an interview? Should I wait until summoned? Or make myself at home? Would I eat with the family or with the servants?

I was on very thin ice and I knew it. My knowledge of medicine was limited to what I had learned in health courses in school and a few phrases I had picked up from my pharmacist friend, Jerry, and from a quick read at the library. If anyone knowledgeable tried to talk medicine with me they would know at once I was a fraud.

I was counting mostly on the brevity of my stay and on Mary Linton's tendency to dispense with practical matters, and her obvious dislike for me, which would surely preclude any unnecessary conversation.

David's presence in the house was an added complication, and he was anything but scatter-brained. I could only hope he was not medically inclined.

Mrs. Evans returned shortly to tell me, "The mistress would like to see you, in her study, if it's convenient. Shall I wait and take you down?"

"You won't have to wait. I've finished unpacking." I felt as ready as I'd ever be to face Mary Linton.

And don't go getting your back up, my girl, I warned myself as I followed Mrs. Evans, she is your employer, if only for a few days, and on top of that she's a dangerous creature. A little servility and some playing dumb will see you through, if you just don't get riled and start behaving foolishly.

I knew as soon as I came into the study that I had made my first gaffe.

"Miss Channing," Mrs. Evans announced and quickly slid by me to disappear down the hall.

He was there as well, standing by the fireplace. His height and the width of his shoulders seemed to dominate the room and even the heavily carved mantle shrank in his presence.

Mary Linton sat in a velvet covered chair, smoking a cigarette in a long, jade holder. She looked surprised at my appearance.

"Is something wrong?" I asked.

"No, only...I somehow expected one of those starched white uniforms and a peaked cap." She blew a cloud of smoke into the room.

My throat felt dry. How incredibly stupid of me. I was supposed to be a nurse, wasn't I?

"I don't ordinarily wear them for house jobs of this sort," I said hastily. "It's been my experience that everyone, especially the patient, is more at ease if I dress in normal fashion."

"In any event," he said from the fireplace, "you look so lovely as you are it would be a shame to bundle you up in starched white."

I felt my face redden. It was an excessive remark, and patronizing. I was dressed rather plainly, in a pale blue shirtwaist, and I did not regard myself as "so lovely."

"If you'd prefer that I wear a uniform," I stammered, speaking to Mary.

She gave a dismissive wave of her hand. "No, that's of no consequence, I'm sure. Have you seen my husband yet?"

Her manner toward me was cold and aloof, more imperious than before. My instinct was to match rudeness with rudeness but I restrained myself and remained placid and servile.

"No, Ma'am, I thought I ought to wait for our interview."

"He's been worse since you were here—when was that?"

"Has he had a doctor?" I asked quickly.

"Of course," she said coldly. "Doctor Mallory, from in town, has been up. He diagnosed it as the flu. I suppose you'll want to consult with him."

Indeed I did not. He would know in an instant I was no nurse. "I don't think that will be necessary at present," I said. "I know the usual procedure to follow with the flu. If it changes, of course, I'll want to talk to him then."

She sighed and put out the cigarette, looking quite bored. "Well, I've instructed the servants to cooperate with you where they can, unless there is something particularly unusual that you'll need." She cocked an eyebrow.

"No, except that I'd like to have charge of his food, if I may." She looked a little surprised by that and I hastened to add, "My training put a great emphasis on the importance of diet in the recuperative process."

"If there's to be a special diet, we ought to get the cook in here and—"

"No, not a special diet, just whatever everyone else is having." I was floundering and think she was beginning think the same thing. I dared not look at the tall man across the room. "That is, I'll look over what she prepared for each meal and pick and choose for him."

"Very well." She hesitated a moment before saying, "I'm not versed in the etiquette for these situations. In your other positions, did you ordinarily eat with the family?" She asked this in a way that indicated she hoped I had not.

I was no more versed in the special etiquette than she was, but I had my preferences. "Sometimes I ate with the help," I said. "But, really, I prefer to eat in my room, if that's not too much trouble."

"Isn't that rather monastic?" David asked. In some odd way he seemed amused by the interview.

"Since I'll be in the kitchen anyway, supervising Mr. Linton's meals, I could easily prepare a tray for myself each time. If someone could bring it up for me."

"Not necessary," he said, in a tone of voice that said he had reached a decision and the matter was entirely settled. "My sister and I have little company at dinner and we shall welcome yours then. Of course if you prefer to have your other meals in your garret room, you may."

"Thank you." I thought of several remarks I would rather have made. Handsome or not, he was the most insufferably overbearing man I had ever known. It was true, I had always wished Jerry, the pharmacist, had a little more backbone, but there was such a thing as too much backbone.

Mary stood from her chair, stretching her long, sleek figure lazily, like a cat. She wore a pants suit in pale green silk. It looked elegant and costly. There was no denying, she was a stunningly beautiful woman. Even had she not been blessed with a vast fortune, I would well understand Jeff's throwing me over as he had. The thought did nothing, however, to increase my fondness for her.

"Mrs. Evans will take you up to my husband's room." She touched a button that brought the housekeeper a moment later, fluttering into the room like an errant moth.

I thanked Mrs. Linton for her time and was on my way out of the room when David spoke again. "One moment, Miss Channing." It was a command and I stopped as ordered, turning back to him.

"I'm a little under the weather myself," he said. "I seem to have acquired a sharp pain here, over the left eye. Can you recommend something for it?"

"Aspirin," I said evenly. "And perhaps some rest."

"Aspirin? I should have thought by this time medical science had come up with something more in the way of pain killer."

"I've no doubt they have." I willed my heart to stop pounding. "But I have no license to prescribe medicines."

"I see." He nodded and I realized I had spoken too quickly. As a nurse I would know for a fact about pain killers, whether I could prescribe them or not.

"I have great faith in aspirin," I said. "Now, if you'll excuse me, I have a patient I should see."

He excused me and I went out in Mrs. Evans' wake. I felt as if I had survived an inquisition. And it would probably not be my last. For whatever reason, David Morgan had not been satisfied with our interview. That pain had come up too quickly, too gratuitously, to be anything but a test.

And I could not but feel I had failed it.

CHAPTER EIGHT

I went directly up to Jeff's room, remembering to let Mrs. Evans show me the way. Jeff was sitting up in bed. I was surprised to see how much better he looked since I had last seen him. Some of the color had returned to his cheeks and his gestures were less tremulous.

Despite the change in his condition, however, he wore a petulant expression as he greeted me and went through the charade of an introduction by Mrs. Evans.

"Miss Channing will be your nurse," the housekeeper explained in a cheery voice. "I expect a pretty young face like hers ought to be a good tonic."

She found her own remark particularly witty and was still chuckling to herself when she left, saying, "I'll leave you to get acquainted."

"I thought you'd come straight here," Jeff said when she was gone.

"I couldn't very well until someone told me where you were. And I've just gone through the new employee interrogation."

He rolled his eyes upward. "Oh, Lord, I didn't think of that. I suppose Mary put you through everything but a blood test."

"Not really. She was cool but that was to be expected. Her brother seemed a little suspicious, though."

"David? He would."

It had occurred to me that someone might come in and think it peculiar that I was standing across the room chatting with the man who was supposed to be my patient. I went to the bed and fussed while we talked, fluffing up a pillow and tilting the lamp-shade so that the light fell less directly into his eyes.

My foot struck something under the bed. "Ouch," I said, stooping down. A large metal strongbox had been shoved under the bed. "What's this, the family jewels?"

"Just some personal papers. Never mind, let's have a look at your foot. I don't want you coming down sick."

"Heavens, I just stubbed my toe. I doubt it will put me in a wheelchair."

"It isn't smart to be flippant about those things. There, put the box way back under. I don't want Mrs. Evans snooping into it. And, no, there aren't any family jewels in it. Nothing more dramatic than copies of my will and some insurance papers, and all the loose cash I've been able to scrape up. I thought we might need that and when we did we'd want it close at hand. It's crude, hiding it under my bed, but since I spend most of my time here it's rather safe, don't you think?"

"Yes, and you're right, it isn't anything to be flippant about. I'm glad you've thought so far ahead." I pushed the metal box well out of the way. "Is he living here? David Morgan, I mean."

"He came for a visit. I have no idea for how long, either. He sometimes likes to look things over at the factory—the glass-works, you know. Just our luck that he would choose this partic-ular time to come."

"He saw me, the last time I was here."

"He didn't." Jeff sat forward, looking alarmed.

"I'm afraid so. We ran into one another. Quite literally, in fact. He was coming in as I was going out. I ran smack into his arms."

"Did he get a look at you?"

"Yes. He remembered me today, too."

"Then I guess that just tears it." Jeff became petulant again. He might have been a small child deprived of some candy instead of a man whose life hung in the balance.

Now that I remembered, though, he had always behaved like a spoiled child. I had overlooked it in the past because I loved him, and as people in love sometimes do, I had even thought it charming. Maybe it had brought out some deep maternal instinct in me.

I only found it annoying now, however, and a bit unmanly to hear his voice too often verging upon a whine. I found myself comparing him almost unconsciously with his brother-in-law.

David Morgan might be annoying, even insulting at times, as such direct people are bound to be, but I felt sure he was not the sort to sulk or whine. In fact, David reminded me of my father. You always knew just where you stood with him.

"Not really," I replied to his dismay over David. "I think I handled it all right. Unless they become suspicious enough to sit down and actually compare dates, they won't likely realize they saw me on two different occasions."

He smiled his approval. "You're right. You know, you're a pretty cool customer in a pinch. I would somehow never have expected it of you." If there was something a little more than simple admiration in his voice I chose not to take notice of it.

"I'd never have expected it myself." I did not add that I had not felt so cool downstairs, under the eyes of the two Morgans. "Anyway, it's all moot. I mean to leave here as soon as possible, a day or two at the most. We've only got to carry it off for that long and everything will be all right."

He sighed deeply. "I wish we could leave that soon."

I had gone idly to the window, pulling the curtain aside, but I turned back to him, startled.

"But aren't we going? I thought that was the whole idea."

"It is, but it's going to take me some time to get my strength back."

"You look better today."

"Not that much better. Can you drive a car?"

"No, I never learned. There's not much point, living in New York."

"And I can't exactly ask Mary or her brother to drive us to the station so we can run away. That means, either I will have to drive us when we go, which I could not possibly manage in my present condition, or we would have to hike it, carrying our bags. It's nearly two miles, even taking the shortest route across the fields."

"I know," I said into the pause. "I walked it the last time."

"And it's getting on to winter. No, my dear, I won't be up to that for a while, I'm quite certain. You do see, don't you?"

He was right, of course. But I hadn't bargained on this. Every day I stayed here increased the risk of my making some mistake and being discovered for the imposter I was. And of course the very real danger existed that, despite my presence, Jeff might be poisoned anyway.

I could keep an eye on the preparation of his food. So long as I saw to it that he ate only what the rest of the family was being served and that no one but I had access to his food once it was dished out, no harm could come to him in that fashion.

I had even thought out how I could take charge of his tea. My excuse was that I had brought with me a special, medicinal tea I believed would help him. No one need know that it was nothing more than ordinary Darjeeling.

How many other ways, however, could poison be administered? I had no idea. I'd had time only for the briefest of reading on arsenic. If Jeff's wife were poisoning him, she had undoubtedly gone into the subject in great detail.

"I know it's unpleasant," he said in a sympathetic voice, "but there's no way around it. Now, why don't you sit and let's get acquainted again, shall we? Don't forget, I've been confined for what seems decades. You're my first honest to goodness visitor. How have you been, and what have you been doing with yourself?"

I would have preferred to return to my own room but better judgment told me it was best to linger for a time. It would not do to have one of the servants whispering downstairs that I had stayed no more than a minute or two in my "patient's" room.

We chatted idly. I carefully steered the conversation away from my personal life. He had forfeited any right to that information five years before. That was not difficult to do. Jeff's favorite subject was himself and once I had brought him around to that, he was safely launched.

He had always been an interesting conversationalist. He told me about some of their travels—quite a bit of travel, apparently, but to someone accustomed to a carefully budgeted vacation once a year, three or four unlimited trips would seem like a constant whirl.

"This last year," he said, actually looking healthier because he was the object of all my attention, "we've stayed pretty close to the hearth. I felt I ought to start taking an interest in the glassworks and I've been poking around there a bit. And then this came along...."

I had a difficult time picturing Jeff, after several years of luxury travel, settling back into the role of businessman. On the other hand, he was inclined to get bored with much of the same thing—or the same person, as I recalled.

After a decent interval, I made my excuses and prepared to retire to my own room.

"You'd better watch out for David," Jeff said thoughtfully. "I'm not entirely certain he isn't in this with Mary."

"That doesn't make much sense, though, does it? I mean, I can see Mary refusing to give you up, but I can hardly imagine David's sharing her possessiveness." I thought, but did not say, I would think if more believable that David did not like him and would be happy to see him go.

"They're like two peas in a pod." He sounded a little piqued at having his opinion challenged. "They'd do anything for one another. Just take my word for it and watch your step with him."

I shrugged and let it lie there. And he was right, to a certain degree. Chances were, if someone were going to guess the truth about me, it would be David and not his sister. Not that Mary was witless, just that she was more inclined to dismiss me as of no consequence. So, yes, I did need to watch my step around David.

Back in my own room, I found myself thinking that I did not much care for Jeff. Love often blinds one to another's true character. We tend to see what romantic idealism has put there instead of what really exists. I have a suspicion that every young woman in love sees the object of her emotions, however ordinary or even ignoble he might be, as Sir Lancelot, a noble and heroic figure.

That was how I had once seen Jeff. Now I saw him in a new, less flattering light. He was not a particularly admirable person. I had to remind myself, of course, that he had been ill and that made people petty and quarrelsome, but I didn't think that was all of it.

It occurred to me, too, that some of Jeff's mistrust of David might be nothing more than jealousy. I didn't fancy that Jeff was still in love with me—I wasn't entirely certain that he ever really had been—but he was the sort who would not like thinking a female, especially one who had been his exclusively, might take an interest in some other man.

David Morgan was an attractive man and Jeff certainly knew that, and knew that I would think so. It was the sort of thing that might rankle, especially since he himself was out of the combat, as it were.

Well, I had not come here for a flirtation with David, or for that matter, with Jeff. I would have been a great deal happier if I weren't here at all, and the prospect of staying for several days, or even weeks, was an unpleasant one.

I had come, though, and taken on the responsibility of getting Jeff safely away from here, and I had been trained from childhood to the idea that when one started a job, one finished it and finished it rightly.

This was the first time, however, that someone's life depended upon how well I did a particular job.

CHAPTER NINE

If I had entertained any illusions that David Morgan had insisted on my dining with the family so that he could dazzle me with his charms, they were quickly dispelled that first evening. Mary was cool to me, beyond asking a few vague questions about her husband's health, and David seemed only dimly aware of my presence. It was not, as was the case with his sister, a snobbish sort of rudeness. He seemed simply preoccupied.

Nor did the brother and sister share a great deal of conversation with one another. They spoke briefly of the Morgan glassworks, with only, "Perhaps you know of the products," for me from David.

To his sister, he said, "I've been looking things over. Everything seems to be going smoothly."

"Jeff took quite an interest in the place for a time. I really rather hoped he'd get genuinely involved with it."

"We have a perfectly good manager there and an understanding that he's to have a free hand." He did not say so but he made it clear that he did not think highly of Jeff's becoming involved with the business.

"Still...." She shrugged it off. "Anyway, he came down sick and that ended that."

They talked a bit more but I had no interest in the Morgan glassworks and I made no effort to follow their conversation.

The dinner was good, the room charming with its paneled walls and gleaming candelabra. We were served by a young woman in her late teens whom I had not seen before. I suppose she came up from town part time.

In addition to her and Mrs. Evans, the staff included a round little woman who cooked and who had a tendency to cross thick hands under thick bosom and study you solemnly when you spoke to her. Another woman, whose name slipped my mind as soon as I heard it, came in days to clean. A man whom I had not met but heard of cared for the grounds and, as I pieced it together, anything outside the house itself, including horses and cars. There had been a maid, as I well knew, but she had in some way displeased Mr. Linton and was let go.

As the meal drew to its close, David seemed to rally from his preoccupation. "I must apologize, Miss Channing," he said, giving me the benefit of a genuinely charming smile, "for our rudeness in discussing something of which you know nothing and in which you have no interest."

"I'm sure it's of great interest to you. It is I who should apologize for my ignorance."

"A beautiful young lady like you should have far more exciting things on her mind than the manufacture of glassware."

"Excitement doesn't always help one earn a living."

He looked about to say something further and changed his mind. Instead, he said to both of us, "How about a liqueur in the study?"

"I think not," Mary said. "The attorneys have sent up a trunkful of papers that need signing. Such a bother when you think how much I pay them to handle these things for me."

"You wouldn't like it if they managed entirely without your supervision," he said with a grin. "You might soon find yourself a pauper."

"Well, the novelists and songwriters say I might be happier. Tell me, Miss Channing, is one happier if one is poor?"

I felt my face redden. "Having never been wealthy," I said a bit more coldly than I should have, "I don't know that I'm qualified to say. But I have known people who really had to struggle just to keep themselves alive and I can't help thinking that they might have been a little happier with just a bit more food in their stomachs."

"Touché." David gave me a mock salute. "After that I insist you at least come and have a liqueur with me. I like a woman who speaks her mind."

I thought, however, as he escorted me to the library, that I would do better to speak my mind a little less where Mary was concerned. It would be awkward if she were to fire me.

"I hope I didn't anger your sister." I accepted the sherry he handed me.

"Mary's accustomed to sparring with other women. In her group, it's a way of life."

For a moment he busied himself lighting the fire in the fire-place. Soon the flames were crackling and dancing, giving off their glow and warmth. He turned his attention back to me.

"You're quite a surprising creature."

"Really?"

"When I heard they were bringing someone in to look after Jeff, I envisioned a grim-faced dragon—particularly knowing my sister as I do. She doesn't usually encourage the company of other women who are attractive."

"You flatter me. I suppose it's easier for a man, but it must be awfully lonely here for Mrs. Linton, particularly if she's accustomed to moving in an active social circle."

He shrugged. "We're both used to spending a part of each year here. To a city dweller like yourself I suppose it does seem isolated and cut off from the world. I thought so myself when I was a child. As a matter of fact, though, that's probably why we both like it now. We have a little bit of money, as you may have guessed, and all the headaches that go with it. Mary's got most of them because our parents rightly thought she had a better head for business than I do. She comes across scatterbrained at times but I assure you anything that has a dollar sign attached to it gets weighed very carefully. And you mustn't think there's nothing to do here. We can manage to keep you entertained."

"I'm not here to be entertained."

He dismissed that as lightly as he did anything that did not seem to fall in line with his way of thinking. "That? Jeff's got a touch of the flu and it's lingering a bit. Not the most serious thing in the world, even you have to admit that. If he weren't such a baby—"

I stood quickly. "Perhaps I'd better excuse myself and retire."

"Oh, Lord, are you going to be one of those?"

"One of what, pray tell?" He had managed, despite my best intentions, to annoy me once again. I couldn't imagine why I reacted so strongly to him.

"One of those females who gets into a snit at everything a man says?" When I started to turn away, he caught my arms. "Okay, look, I'm sorry. If I promise to speak of nothing more serious than the weather, will you stay a little longer, please?"

"I will accept the apology, and I should offer one of my own. But it has been a long day for me and frankly, I'm a little tired. If you'll excuse me, I really would like to go to bed."

"Fair enough, so long as we aren't parting on that frosty note, and on one condition—tomorrow you let me show you around a little."

"I really ought...."

"I know, you aren't here for a vacation, but no one said you had to be a household slave, either. Look, Jeff's been doing a lot of resting and sleeping, which I suspect you will agree is good for him. There's no reason why we can't have a look around while he's asleep, is there?"

"Well, if you're sure it will be all right...." It might even, I was thinking, be useful if I knew the lay of the land.

"You mean with Mary? Leave her to me, all right?"

"All right. And now I will excuse myself. Good night, Mister Morgan."

He snapped his fingers as if remembering something suddenly. "Almost forgot, there is one thing I will insist upon while you're here."

"And that is...?"

"That you call me David, and not Mr. Morgan."

"Oh." I was genuinely surprised. "I don't think that's the

ordinary thing...."

"Neither of us is an ordinary person," he said softly.

Our eyes met and I had an awful moment of self-discovery and a warning voice sounded in my ear, saying, careful, girl, you can't afford to think thoughts like that about this man, of all the men in the world.

I forced my eyes away from his. "I think you may be mistaken about me. I'm afraid I am altogether ordinary. But I will defer to your wishes, David."

"Thank you, Chris—it is Chris, isn't it, and not Christmas?"

"Yes, it is. And now good night."

The fire had been lit in my room too, to cast dancing shadows on the walls. I went to the window and looked out upon the moonlit scene. The distant woods looked eerie. The window glass was cold to my touch. The room smelled faintly of the burning logs.

After a long time I came from the window and undressed, slipping into the warm and quite unglamorous flannel nightgown in which I always slept. I turned out the lights and got into bed, staring up at the patterns cast on the ceiling by the low-burning fire.

CHAPTER TEN

In the morning I saw to Jeff's breakfast and had my own in the safety of my bedroom. Jeff was again petulant.

"What will you do with yourself all day?" he asked.

"Dav...Mr. Morgan has offered to show me around the estate."

He scowled. "I don't like that. I'll bet he's up to something."

I couldn't resist smiling. Not even Jeff's sour mood could dampen my spirits this morning. I had awakened to a golden dawn, almost literally with a song in my heart.

"I shouldn't be surprised," I replied. "Men often are, I've been told."

Which did not brighten his mood at all. "Listen, don't be taken in by that phony charm of his. I've seen him operate before. But it doesn't necessarily mean anything, he may just be planning to pump you for information. Anyway, he's not the sort of man a woman should trust."

And you are, I suppose, I thought wryly but did not say it. "Well, I can hardly refuse his invitation without risking his displeasure, and that might not be wise at this point in time."

"If only I could get out of this bed," he said, wriggling impatiently.

"If you could we would be on our way to New York City, but you can't. Your job right now is to stay in it and recover as quickly as possible. My job is to keep anyone from getting suspicious and discovering the truth. That is the reason I accepted the invitation to go exploring with Mr. Morgan." I saw no need to mention any other reasons.

David was waiting when I came down the stairs in mid-morning. He looked as if he had been waiting for a time but he restrained whatever impatience he felt.

"Better bundle up," he said. "It's cold out there this morning."

It was indeed cold, but nicely so. I have always rather enjoyed a brisk, clear winter morning with the sun playing hide-and-seek behind some drifting clouds.

"In the summer," he said, escorting me around the front terraces, "these are planted with flowers. Very colorful, although I'm afraid I couldn't begin to tell you the names of any of them."

"It must be lovely."

"Maybe you'll be here to see them."

"I hope not," I said without thinking, and added hastily, "I should hate to think your brother-in-law's flu would linger that long."

He laughed and said, "If it would keep you here until spring I'd be tempted to slip something into his food, just to keep him in bed."

I had to force a laugh in response. "I'm afraid that wouldn't reflect very well on the care he'd gotten. And I do have to work for a living."

"So you're set to be a career girl for life? No plans for marriage, little vine-covered cottage, husband and children?"

I wondered what he would say if I told him who that husband had almost been, but I had no intention of telling him that.

The woods lay before us across an open field. "Is there a stream there?" I asked, changing the subject pointedly.

He laughed but took it in good form. "Yes, there is."

"With a pond?"

"You mean a for-skating pond? Yes, there is. Would you like to see it?"

"I would, please."

We walked in silence across the field, picking our way carefully through frozen ruts and tracks. "We let one of our neighbors farm our fields. This was corn last summer, and I remember some kind of grain. I'm afraid I'm not much of a farmer."

A few corn shocks—bundles of dried stalks—still stood here and there, lending a Currier and Ives quality to the scene. I had spent parts of two summers with an aunt on her Ohio farm, but not enough time to be much more of a farmer than he was.

A short distance into the woods we came to the stream, now frozen over. It followed a circuitous path, widening a little further along into a pond that I thought would serve very well for ice-skating.

"Think it will do?" he asked.

"It's not Rockefeller Place, but it's quite lovely. But I didn't bring my skates.

The woods lay behind and to the right of us. To the left and before us were hills, with a steeply cut bluff bordering the pond on its other side. The tranquil beauty was too relaxing. It would be difficult here to remember to guard what one said and did.

"I suppose we ought to start back," I said.

"Some of these outbuildings are as old as the hills," he said when we were approaching the house again. "Those sheds are for storage and that was originally a summer kitchen and a spring house, back before the days of refrigerators. The garages, of course, are much newer, and that building way over there is a guest house, although I can't think when it was last used."

All of the buildings except the garages were made of stone and I would have been hard pressed to say which were older than the others. The estate had a sprawling look despite the massive solidity of the house itself.

"May I see the stables?" I asked. "If it isn't too much bother. Are there horses?"

"Do you ride?"

"A little, yes."

We walked the rest of the way in silence, an air of constraint settling between us. I was afraid every moment of what I might say that would give me away as an imposter, while he seemed to have lost some of his blatant self-confidence.

At the stables, however, we both seemed to forget our reserve, perhaps because we simply became less aware of one another.

I had never seen better horses than those in the Morgan stables.

"Are they Morgans?" I asked. Morgan horses were a famous breed descended from Justin Morgan.

"Only Daisy, coincidentally." He indicated one lovely light saddle horse. But the others were fine animals as well. We went to each one in turn, David explaining the fine points of each. We patted and made a fuss over them and I was pleased to see that they welcomed him. Animals' instincts are often sound and it was evident from their manner toward him that he was kind to them. Without quite knowing why, I was pleased to make that discovery.

I might be unsophisticated about many things but I knew horses, and I did not hesitate to speak frankly about these, even going so far as to disagree with him once or twice. Far from annoying him, this seemed to please him, and he treated me with a new respect.

"Jupiter," I said, patting one particularly beautiful stallion. I caressed the soft, silky neck. David had warned me that he was hard to hold, but I had no difficulty. "I'd love to race across the hills with you, you beauty."

"Why not?" David asked. "It never occurred to me that you would want to ride, but you're welcome to. I could use some company, as a matter of fact."

"Oh, I couldn't." I suddenly remembered my place here. "Your sister—"

"Hardly ever rides. The poor beasts are sadly neglected. You'd be doing them and me a favor to make some use of them. How about this afternoon?"

"I have a patient to consider," but I knew my voice lacked conviction. I did want to ride, regardless of what my better judgment told me, and I knew he could hear it in my voice.

"He sleeps during the afternoon. We would only be out for an hour or so." And when I continued to hesitate, he said in a more authoritative voice, ""It's settled. We'll go out this afternoon. Do you have riding clothes with you? Well, don't worry about that. Mrs. Evans will come up with something. Leave everything to me." He beamed like a small boy who has been promised a special treat.

I found myself thinking how wonderful it would be to truly leave everything in his hands. What confidence he inspired, as if there were nothing he couldn't resolve satisfactorily. But my greatest problem, of course, I could not turn over to him.

"We'd better go back," I said. The walls had come up between us again.

"If we'd been needed someone would have been out looking for us."

"I'm here to look after your brother-in-law, not to enjoy a vacation."

Despite the coolness of the air, the sun was warm on my shoulders as we strolled back toward the house. "I so love horses," I said on an impulse.

"I prefer them to people."

"Have you had such an unhappy life?"

"I've been unhappy." If he thought my question impertinent he did not seem to mind. "I suppose if the truth were told I was a rude, tiresome little brat who deserved to be lonely in an isolated mansion. I thought this a lonely place then."

For the first time I suddenly thought of him as a human being, a person like any other, who could be lonely or sad or hurt. In a flash of insight I saw through the mask of arrogance he assumed, and saw the man within. In the same moment I felt a strange sensation within my breast, as though a tiny arrow had pierced my heart.

"Is something wrong?"

I had been staring at him without realizing it. I was embarrassed at having been so open.

"No," I said, trying to hide my emotion, but he stopped abruptly and, seizing my arm, brought me to a halt as well.

"I don't believe that you are a nurse at all."

I had to fight back a wave of panic. Somehow I managed to look up and meet his eyes. "What...what do you mean?"

"I think you're a sorceress and you've come here for the sole purpose of bewitching me and turning me into your slave." A faint smile played at the corners of his mouth.

"Oh," I said stupidly. A flood of contradictory emotions washed over me—relief that he had only been joking, a thrill of happiness at the hint in his words, confusion, and fear that he might be secretly laughing at me.

I don't know what else I might have said but at that moment fate in the person of Mrs. Evans intervened. The back door opened and she stepped out.

"Begging your pardon," she called, "but Mr. Linton is awake and has been asking for you, Miss."

David let go of me and I, unable to think of anything to say and not sure I could trust my voice to say it, turned from him and hurried toward the back steps.

CHAPTER ELEVEN

Mr. Morgan was a man of his word. I was still eating lunch in my room when Mrs. Evans appeared with an armful of clothes.

"Mr. Morgan said you would be wanting a riding habit, Miss," she said, "I think I have everything here and as near as I can judge, they ought to fit you well."

She did indeed have a complete riding costume, down to a pair of very expensive looking boots. "Are these Mrs. Linton's clothes?" I asked, fingering the excellent fabric. I had always ridden in ordinary slacks before or even jeans. I had never had the extra money for jodhpurs.

"I couldn't say, Miss."

Her evasiveness, however, told me that they had come from someone other than Mrs. Linton. And the sizes seemed not quite right for her.

Well, what of it, I asked myself? David was a handsome man and wealthy to boot. It should come as no surprise to find that at some time or other he had entertained a woman here at this house, had known her well enough and often enough that she apparently kept some clothes here and had never retrieved all of them. Probably she was of the social set that would not regard the loss of a few changes of costume and a riding habit of any great significance.

Nevertheless I found myself wondering about her—how long ago had it been since she was here, whether she had been as good a horsewoman as I, whether they had been in love....

David was waiting when I came down. He gave a low whistle

when he saw me. "If I'm any guess," he said, "you ride like you were born to the saddle."

"I think I do fairly well, although my experience has been limited for the most part to Central Park."

"You must have turned a few heads."

"You flatter me. Most of the young women I rode with were as good as I, if not better."

It was a marvelous morning for riding. The air was cold and sharp. The horses seemed to have been anticipating our arrival and I could easily imagine they were excited at the prospect of a run.

"He's certainly taken to you," David said when I mounted Jupiter with no difficulty. The horse was spirited, but quick to respond to my slightest wish. "Which," David added, "increases my respect for his judgment."

I let David take the lead. He started slowly, making certain that I was capable before he let his own mount out.

"You needn't be afraid," I called to him. "We can keep up."

He laughed, accepting the challenge, and in a flash we were galloping across the fields skirting the woods. He did not even glance back to see that I was with him and I took that as a vote of confidence.

"All right, you darling," I said to Jupiter, "let's have a real run of it, shall we?"

He gave his head a toss as if he had understood and welcomed the challenge. I could feel the muscles stretch and flex in his powerful sides. A laugh of delight escaped my lips, caught on the wind, and was carried away behind me.

The air was crisp in my face. Jupiter carried me magnificently. I felt as if we had wings as we flew over the rough, frozen ground. We took a small fence and left the fringes of the wood, taking again to the open ground. A single tree stood, silhouetted starkly against the gray of the sky. I felt a wild excitement mounting within me with every thud of the stallion's hooves.

I was scarcely aware of David streaking before me, his coat a flash of red. He rode well, very well. I began to pay more attention to him. He might have been riding Pegasus himself. I pushed Jupiter a little harder but David stayed well ahead of me, riding truly as if he were part of his mount.

The field of stubble sloped downhill. Ahead of us lay a high hedge, bare of leaves but so thick that it made a wall anyway and high enough that one could not see over it on the approach. I knew that jumping blind could be dangerous and I watched to see what David would do.

He went straight for it. For a moment horse and rider made a tableau, framed against the sky in an attitude of grace before they disappeared from view.

We came up to the hedge, Jupiter soaring into the air with ease. I saw a ditch on the other side, veering away from the hedge at the point where David had jumped, but too close to the spot where we were crossing to be taken safely.

There was no time to do anything, scarcely time to see the trap waiting for us and to realize what was going to happen.

Then we were tumbling over. I seemed to be falling up into the sky. The ground rushed toward me. A scream that must have been my own, and the moment of impact.

Then darkness.

CHAPTER TWELVE

I regained consciousness in his arms. I looked up into his handsome face, concern written across it.

It must have been the bump on the head because I had really promised myself I would not fall in love with him. Yet, here I was, and I could not tell which had me so dazed—the fall or the sight of his face so close to mine.

"Are you all right?" he asked.

"I...I think so. I didn't see the ditch in time."

"My fault. I forgot it was there. I always cross further up, where it's safe. I just didn't think...."

"You mustn't blame yourself. It was stupid of me. I should have crossed where you did." I tried to sit up but the ground suddenly swooped and swerved again.

He steadied me with his arm about me. "Don't try to move for a minute. You got a nasty bump."

"Jupiter...?"

I knew from the way he avoided my eyes that Jupiter must have broken a leg. "Oh, David," I said, heartsick. I heard a soft whinny and looked in its direction. One glance confirmed my fears.

"It's all right," he said, "don't think about it."

His own horse, a gray, stood obediently nearby. "Do you think you can ride if I put you on Miranda? I could walk you back to the house that way."

"Yes, I think so. I don't think there are any bones broken. But what about Jupiter?"

"I'll send Raymond back." He brought his horse over and lifted me up into the saddle as if I weighed nothing. I still felt weak and a little dizzy, but I had made an effort to sit upright. I had already made enough of a fool of myself and cost him one of his best horses, with my careless riding. I looked back at the fallen horse as we set out, but there was nothing I could do in that quarter. I brushed a tear from my eye. Dear, beautiful Jupiter, suffering for my mistake.

Mrs. Evans saw us coming and rushed out to hold the door and cluck at us while David carried me in his strong arms.

"Take her up straight up," Mrs. Evans gave him orders as if she were mistress here and he the servant. "Right up to her room. I'll be there right behind you with some tea and brandy."

I closed my eyes, thinking how wonderful it was to be in his arms like this, to rest my head against his powerful chest. My arms were about his neck and I could smell the clean, masculine scent of him and feel a lock of dark hair brushing the back of one hand.

I did not try, in my dazed condition, to tell myself these were dangerous thoughts. For this brief space in time I was no cautious, reasoning creature. I was a helpless woman in the strong and capable arms of a protecting male, the man I loved. It was, I confess, a delicious feeling despite my condition.

Mrs. Evans came with the tea, steaming hot and the brandy. David, his strength and protection having served their immediate purposes, was sent away and the housekeeper took over, getting me out of the riding habit and into my nightgown and my bed.

"I'll be all right now, I'm sure," I said.

She clucked. "The only thing for a bad fall is some tea and some brandy and a spell in bed. Now under those covers with you, that's the girl."

So I allowed myself to be fussed over, pampered and bundled into bed and, much to my surprise, probably as a result of the unaccustomed brandy, I fell asleep almost at once.

I woke when Mrs. Evans came into the room carrying a tray

with some warm supper on it. The darkened windows informed me it was evening.

"There you are, awake," she greeted me, beaming maternally. "Feeling better?"

I stretched my arms a bit tentatively. "A little stiff and sore, but otherwise fine."

"Mr. Morgan said I was to let him know the minute you woke up, but I said you might want to eat first."

"Thank you. I would like to get into my clothes and freshen up."

"He says you're to stay in bed, Miss, and not to worry about anything or anyone." She did not spell it out, but she delivered the message in such a way as to tell me, from David, that I wasn't to worry about Mary's reaction to my being abed.

That was not, however, what was worrying me. "Thank you for your concern," I said, throwing the covers back determinedly, "but I really do want to be up. I've never much cared for just lying about."

"Very well, Miss, I'm sure." She went out looking a little offended at having her well-meant advice ignored.

I had barely dressed and made myself presentable when David knocked at the door and, at my bidding, came in. He still wore an expression of grave concern.

"You ought to have stayed in bed," he said. "No one was going to scold you."

"And next thing you'll be hiring a nurse to look after me," I said with a laugh. Then, growing sober, I said, "David, I'm so awfully sorry about Jupiter."

"You're to put that straight out of your head," he said in a firm voice. "And that's an order. I just thank the Lord that you weren't hurt."

"Your sister could always find another nurse," I said to tease him.

"Not like you," he said in such a serious voice that my smile faded.

"I think I ought to look in on Jeff." I was suddenly embarrassed by what I saw in his eyes. I tried to move past him but he was having none of that. He seized me in his arms.

"Do you do this to every man you meet?" His voice was hoarse.

"I don't know what you mean." My heart pounded.

"Hasn't anyone ever told you that you're beautiful?"

His face was so near mine, his lips parted, his eyes searching mine longingly. I felt as if the room, the entire world, had melted away and in all the universe there was nothing but his wonderful face before me and the hands that held me so firmly.

"Don't be silly." I tried without success to laugh. "I'm a very plain-looking woman with...."

"With very bad eyesight. That first time, when you ran into me at the door, I had just a glimpse of you and it was like a vision sent from heaven. Those magnificent eyes of yours, so frightened looking, those lips, that no man could see without wanting to kiss...." He bent to kiss me.

"No." I twisted away. "I...I don't think we should talk like this." I had remembered, almost too late, who he was and who I was, and why I was here. I dared not give myself up to the emotions that were racing through me. I must remain on my guard, even though every fiber of my being was screaming at me to trust him, to believe the words he said.

"Why not, for Pete's sake?" he demanded angrily. But he had released me and I was able to move away from him, breathing heavily. And distance gave me some protection from the spell he had cast over me.

I shook my head. "I...please, let's not. We just mustn't."

"What complete nonsense. I'm here practically at your feet, telling you how I feel, how the very sight of you dazzles me and that I haven't been able to think of anything else...."

"No, don't." I put my hands to my ears as if I could blot out the sound of his voice.

For a moment he looked at me with such anger that I wouldn't have been surprised if he had struck me. Then, turning on his heel, he went out, banging the door shut.

I sank down upon my bed, heartsick. If only I could have trusted him, if only there were no barriers between us....

After a time I grew calm again and things fell into more orderly patterns in my mind. Of course there were barriers between us. I had put them there. I sat up, drying my eyes. What reason had I for distrusting David? None, except that he was Mary's brother. And he didn't like Jeff. Well, what of that? I didn't like him a great deal myself.

In point of fact, if one put all the facts down in a black and white fashion, I had only the slimmest of reasons for suspecting anyone of something so drastic as murder. There had been arsenic in Jeff's tea, and he was indeed sick, and the symptoms were those of arsenic poisoning.

Very well, those were facts, but everything else was fancy, based on suspicion and dislike. I did not like Mary Linton and so I had been quick to side with Jeff, to accept his suspicions as my own. Yes, I could see that she had a motive, but if motives were all, most men would be murderers.

"I ought not to have come here," I told my reflection in the mirror. Perhaps after all it would be best if I dropped my little bomb, told David and Mary and the local law enforcement officers exactly who I was and what I was doing here. Let the pieces fall where they may.

After all, regardless of how the local police might want to side with Mary, and even assuming she really was trying to murder Jeff, she could hardly go ahead and do so once that hue and cry had been sounded, could she? And I could be on my way back to Manhattan free from the entangling web of deception and distrust.

I went to the mirror to repair my face. Then I slipped from my room and across the hall, to Jeff's. He was awake, sitting up in his bed. He greeted me sourly.

"Well, I'm glad to see you didn't forget about me altogether."

I ignored the sarcasm. "I suppose someone told you I had an accident."

"Yes. I'm glad, of course, you weren't seriously hurt. But it does make one thing clear, wouldn't you say?"

"What do you mean?"

"Why, about David. We wondered whether he was in this with Mary or not. And now we know."

I shrank back, the implication becoming horribly clear. "I don't see how we can...it was an accident."

"Was it?" He fixed his eyes coldly on me and I felt certain he saw some of the emotions churning within me. "I don't think so. He knows every rut and track in those fields. He knew just where it was safe to cross that hedge and just where it couldn't be done without a nasty fall, a fall that might have broken your neck if you weren't a fine horsewoman."

I tried to tell myself that this wasn't so. It could have been purely accidental, a result of my own carelessness and his—his, the assumption of someone thoroughly familiar with the land, assuming that everyone else shared his knowledge. Simply not thinking until it was too late.

But I could not altogether deny Jeff's suggestion. A mediocre horsewoman could have been killed in a fall like that. And David had done nothing to steer me away from that part of the hedge, hadn't tried to warn me....

"I...I'll fix your supper," I said, trying to fix my confused senses on something real and tangible.

"It isn't necessary. I've eaten."

I had started toward the door but I now turned back to him. His words had been weighted and I saw now, for the first time, the tray on the stand by his bed.

"Mary fixed my dinner for me. I couldn't refuse to eat it, could I?"

I tried to tell myself it meant nothing, that the fear I saw on his face in that moment was unjustified, but I suppose some other part of me knew the truth. I was not surprised when Jeff took dreadfully ill during the night.

"Miss, Miss." Mrs. Evans' voice and her insistent knocking roused me from the fitful sleep into which I had fallen. "You'd better come, quick. The mister is in an awfully bad way. I think he may be done for."

CHAPTER THIRTEEN

I had not come totally unprepared. I knew enough from a hasty afternoon reading at the library to administer emetics. I thought the vomiting alone must surely kill a man, and after that, on the advice of a dubious Jerry in New York, I gave him fluids, all the fluids that Mrs. Evans and I could get into him. It was perhaps crude and all the while that we struggled to bring him back from the brink, I had to pretend a professionalism that I did not possess.

Blessedly Mrs. Evans was as efficient and cool as any nurse I had ever seen. Moreover, she kept Mary and David out of the room altogether, informing them in no uncertain terms that they would only be in the way. So I had her alone to watch me and if she saw that I was less than skilled at this, she kept that to herself.

However crude our efforts might have been, they worked. When I first came into the room with her, dressed in nothing but my nightgown, I too thought he was surely going to die. Nothing in my past experience had prepared me for the sight of a man in so bad a way as this. And for a time I continued to think that our efforts were in vain, that he would surely die while we struggled to save him.

Gradually, however, our work began to reap rewards. Just as I was about to admit defeat and send one of the servants for the doctor, we saw some color return to his face and his movements became less convulsive. The attack was passing.

By morning he was sleeping quietly. He looked utterly

wasted, almost dead, in fact, but I knew that he would live. Mrs. Evans was of the same mind.

"I think that's got it," she said, wiping a hand wearily across her brow. She looked haggard and exhausted and I felt certain that I looked no better, but for a moment as we looked at one another across a sleeping Jeff, we shared a glow of triumph. I think I must have felt what a real nurse or doctor felt when they saved a life. Never had life seemed so precious, so wonderful a thing to me.

David was in the hall outside. He had brought a chair up and was dozing. He sat up as we came out, awake instantly.

"Is he...?" he asked and hesitated.

"He's had a very rough time," I said, "but he's going to be all right now."

I meant that most sincerely. My carelessness had nearly cost him his life. I could not even think of going now. I was under every obligation to protect the life I had saved tonight.

"He's going to be all right thanks to this young lady," Mrs. Evans said. "Thank the Lord she was here. I wouldn't have given you two cents for his life when he rang the bell and I came up earlier."

"We'd better tell Mary," David said.

"Is she up?" I asked. I had seen no sign of her since Mrs. Evans had banished her from the sick room.

"Did you think she was going off to bed?" David asked.

"I...I don't know," I said frankly. "People react to these things differently."

"She's in the study. Do you want to come with me?"

I was quite exhausted but I sensed that he wanted me t come with him to tell Mary. "All right," I said.

Afterward, I thought it was because he wanted me to see that his sister was not all veneer, that beneath her coldly sophisticated exterior she too had feelings.

It was good for me to see that. I had envied and hated her for years without seeing her. And I would never care for her. But for the first time, as we came into the study, I saw her as a real, thinking and feeling human being. She was a woman afraid and greatly concerned for her husband.

I realized what I had never grasped before—she truly loved Jeff. Perhaps it was a possessive, destructive love that would see him dead before she would lose him to another, but there was no doubt in my mind of the depth of her feeling for him.

Her face was ashen as we came in, her eyes wide. She too had spent a sleepless night, perhaps a harder one than mine, for while I had worked, she could only wait, which of course was the hardest task of all.

"Is he...?" She couldn't finish the question.

"He's going to be all right," I said.

"Oh, God!" She began to sob, covering her face with her hands.

David gave me a grateful look and went to her, putting protective arms about her. I left them and went wearily up to my own room.

That one glimpse of Mary Linton as a flesh-and-blood woman was apparently all that I was to see. By midday, when I saw her again, she was as self-possessed as ever and, if possible, more imperious than before. It was as if she resented my having seen her moment of weakness.

I woke about noon after an all-too-brief sleep. My first thought was of Jeff. Through my foolishness I had nearly caused his death. I did not intend to repeat that mistake. Hereafter I meant to keep a very close eye indeed on everything that concerned him.

When I had finished with our lunches and came downstairs again, it was to find Mary dressed for travel. She called my name as I descended the stairs, summoning me into her study with all the authority she could put into her voice.

"I want to thank you for your efforts last night," she said, but these words of gratitude were delivered in such a thankless manner that I felt more as if I had been reprimanded. "Mrs. Evans told me it was your skill and efficiency that pulled him through."

"That is why I am here." I was none too charming myself. As usual she had managed to put my back up.

"He'll be all right now?"

"I should think so. He's had a bad setback, of course, and it's going to mean another week or so in bed, but I think I can safely say he's going to recover."

She seemed to consider that for a moment and I wondered if she had taken it as a warning of some sort.

"I have urgent business that takes me into the city," she said with what I thought was a trace of apology in her voice. "Of course, had my husband's condition remained critical I would have stayed here, but I am no asset in such situations. Indeed, I seem to be more in the way. I think it just as well to leave him in your capable hands."

I hesitated briefly. Why should she feel it necessary to explain to me, or offer what might have been a veiled apology? Then, seeing through her sophisticated armor, I thought I understood—in her aloof way she was asking my blessing on her going. She wanted to be reassured that it was all right for her to do so.

"Mr. Linton's condition is greatly improved this morning," I said, stretching the truth a little, "and as you say, there's nothing you could accomplish by remaining. Right now he needs rest."

"Very well." She gave me the ghost of a smile. As I started from the room, she added, "I had no idea what a difference you were going to make here."

"I hope any change has been to the good." I was thinking, she surely could not yet know how great the difference was going to be before I finished.

I alternated between Jeff's room and my own throughout the afternoon. For the most part, he slept. Gradually the color returned to his face and his eyes, when he was awake, had lost that dull glaze that had seemed to see beyond the grave.

With evening I went to the kitchen, where the cook studied me solemnly as I dished out Jeff's dinner. I even made a point of tasting several things directly from the pot. If by any stretch of the imagination she knew anything about poison, I thought this would serve as a warning to her.

Which, upon reflection, I decided was silly. She could hardly poison the entire dinner without killing off everyone in the household and not just Jeff.

When Jeff had eaten I took his things back down to the kitchen. I ought to have had dinner myself but I was not really hungry, and I went back to my room, thinking I would have something cold later.

I had not been there long when a knock sounded at the door and I opened it to find David standing there.

"I've come to bring you down to dinner," he said with a little bow.

"Thank you, but I thought I'd just wait and have something in the kitchen later."

"Like a scullery maid?" he asked with a twinkle in his eye. When I did not respond, he asked, "What's wrong?"

"Nothing, except I forgot that I was here for a job and went off gallivanting, and as a result my patient nearly died. I think that in the future I ought to take my work a little more seriously."

"I don't see that Jeff's taking sick again is your fault." Of course, if he didn't know about the poison, he wouldn't understand what I meant. "And even if it were, there's no logical reason to punish yourself by hiding in your room. I'm sure if you ask him he would want you to be as comfortable here as possible. Certainly I do, and so does my sister."

"I'm quite comfortable in my room."

"Then I shall have to appeal to your compassion and throw myself upon your mercy."

"I haven't the faintest idea what you mean."

"Quite simply, my sister is gone and unless you come down I shall have to eat alone, which I particularly dislike doing. To make things even worse, by the time we've finished all this arguing, everything will be stone cold, which I also dislike."

I could not help smiling. He was so determined, and the

coaxing in his voice so convincing, I felt my resistance melting.

"Well, if it's really so important...."

"It is." His pleasure at having won his way lighted up his entire face.

To my surprise, we did not go down to the dining room, but into a small room beyond, which I had not seen it before.

It was a lovely room. Unlike the dining room, whose walls were wood-paneled, these were covered in silk. The room was lit with candles in shining crystal. A fire burned on the hearth, before which stood a pair of small sofas.

A table had been set for two, gleaming with silver and crystal and fine China. A bowl of red roses sat in the center. It was cozy and charming, yet still elegant.

The kitchen maid came in response to the bell. She poured wine while David seated me at the table. Soft music played somewhere close at hand.

The maid went out, and David took his seat across for me, smiling in a mysterious way. I was not much of a drinker, but the wine seemed fitting, and I lifted my glass.

"A toast." He raised his glass also, "to my beautiful companion."

I sipped my wine. "This is such a lovely room," I said, glancing around again, "I can't help thinking it's a shame not to use it more often."

He seemed to find this remark amusing. "We call it the lovers' room. I had a great uncle who was something of a rake. He reserved this room for romantic occasions."

"Then it hardly seems appropriate for us to eat here," I said naively. I looked into his dark eyes and saw a faint hint of amusement. Suddenly I saw what he meant and my cheeks turned crimson. I thought he must be laughing at me.

He reached across the table to take my hand, and said, "I don't know how I can put it any more plainly. I love you."

CHAPTER FOURTEEN

The maid came in to remove our dishes. I hardly knew what I had eaten or if I had eaten at all. I was dazed.

"We'll be more comfortable over here by the fire," he said, leading me to one of the velvet sofas. Something within me told me I should excuse myself but I could not. I felt embarrassed and shy I with him. I didn't dare put a name to the other emotions I was feeling.

"You're awfully quiet tonight," he said.

"Am I?" I couldn't remember any of the conversation since he had said, "I love you." I suppose we must have spoken but none of it lingered in my consciousness.

The maid left with the last of the serving things and we were alone, the two of us, in that romantic chamber. I thought the pounding of my heart must be audible throughout the house, telling everyone of my consternation. He poured himself a drink, offering me one, which I refused with a shake of my head. I needed nothing more to intoxicate me.

He stood by the fireplace, resting an arm on the mantle, and watching me. I had to look away from him for fear he might laugh at my confusion.

"I fell in love with you that first time," he said softly, as though the conversation had gone on without interruption, "when we ran into one another at the door."

"I don't think we ought to be talking like this." Even to my own ears, my voice sounded unconvincing. I couldn't help it. No matter what my reason told me, I wanted to listen, wanted to hear these things. I had never known that the mere sound of a voice could fill me with such emotion, could make me shiver as if I had been touched in a sensitive spot. I had thought I knew the thrill of love before, with Jeff, but I had been little more than a child. Nothing I had experienced before was like this.

"I thought you were only being modest," he went on as if I had not objected, "but I finally came to realize that you really don't know how beautiful you are. That day, in the gray light, your eyes wide, I expected you to be, I'm not sure what, self-possessed, I suppose. But you always seem to be so vulnerable. I feel the need to protect you."

Suddenly he knelt before me. I tried to look away, but he put his hands on my shoulders and said, "Look at me."

I raised my eyes, looking straight into his. The fire I saw blazing there seemed to light a path into the very depths of my heart. I was spellbound. It was not only his hands that held me, but some sort of magnetism against which I was powerless.

"I love you," he said again. "Nothing else matters to me. Let's go away from here, the two of us. I have money. Mary can hire another nurse. We can go to Europe, to the Caribbean—anywhere you want to go, as long as I'm with you."

My senses returned to me then and I saw the trap into which I was rushing. "No, please," I managed to say, "we can't."

He let me go. I took a deep breath, trying to sound as businesslike as possible, despite the throbbing of my pulse.

"Why on earth can't we?" he demanded. "I love you and you love me."

"I've never said that."

He smiled at me. "Do you think you need to say it in so many words? Do you think I don't already know you, just because we met recently? I can see it in the way you look at me, in the way you turn your head, in the light burning in your eyes right now, in the way you part your lips when you're happy or excited."

"Aren't you forgetting who I am? I'm a paid employee here." I stood, trying to regain some bit of calm.

He stood too. "I have forgotten. I've forgotten everything

except that you're a woman, the woman I love and want, and that we're alone here together, and may never be again, the way you're acting."

I tried to leave but that was futile. He seized me again, gently, but with an authority that would not let me escape. His arms went about me, drawing me close.

For a moment more I was afraid, I wanted to flee, but his arms were a citadel that imprisoned me, and the next moment his lips were on mine, and all thought of escape fled from me. I forgot who we were, why I was here, all the danger that haunted me. I forgot how to resist or object. I forgot that the world existed beyond his lips.

I soared upward, into the golden light, into the sun itself. I felt its power surge through me, felt its heat burning me, and within me an answering flame burst into life. It seemed an eternity later that are lips parted.

"Darling," he murmured.

I could say nothing, only bury my face against his wide shoulder. He bent his head, kissing my shoulder, my throat, my cheek, my hair.

"I love you," he whispered over and over.

I knew I must resist, must stop this before it was beyond control, but instead I stood within the circle of his arms, trembling at the kisses raining upon me, filled with an ecstasy I had never known before.

He put a hand under my chin and tilted my face to look deep into my eyes. "You're mine," he said, "forever." He kissed me again more passionately than before, and again I felt that sense of hopelessness beneath his lips, that soaring into the heights.

But I knew I must stop this at any cost. He was wild with love and desire. I managed to gasp, "I must go."

"Never."

I did what I knew must be done. I lifted a hand and slapped him as hard as I could.

His astonishment was so great I was able in one quick movement to escape his embrace, staggering away from him to stand on the other side of the velvet sofa. Behind him the fire still burned. The soft music still played. It was incredible that the world did not change at all, except in my heart.

"What on earth?" he said, stupefied, "what's wrong?"

To my horror I began to cry, tears streaming down my cheeks. "I'm sorry," I said, sobbing, "please, excuse me."

I threw open the door and ran into the hall. I was grateful there was no one about to see my sobbing flight up the stairs to my own room. He made no move to stop me. I locked the door to my room behind me, knowing even as I did so that it was foolish.

He would not be coming for me. I had hurt him far beyond the force of that one slap. And I had hurt myself too, more than he would ever know.

What else could I have done? How could I tell him the man he thought was my patient was once my fiancé? How could I explain that his sister was trying to murder her husband? That Jeff thought he was an accomplice? That I half- believed he had tried to kill me by letting my horse take a fall. That I could not fully believe his protestations of love because I feared they were only a way to gain my confidence?

I stumbled across the room to my bed, throwing myself across it and crying with all the force of a broken heart.

CHAPTER FIFTEEN

I did not see David until late the following morning, but shortly after I had awakened, I received a note delivered by Mrs. Evans.

"Forgive me," it read, in a bold masculine hand, "for having taken so many liberties. I was rude and presumptuous, and I would hardly be surprised to learn you're packing your things at this very moment. But I would be very unhappy if I drove you away. I beg you to stay on and to accept my humble apologies."

I folded the note carefully and put it into my dresser drawer, pretending that I did not see Mrs. Evans' curiosity. There was no reply I can safely make to it. Of course I must accept his apologies, but I can hardly tell him they were unnecessary, that it was I who should apologize. He had not been presumptuous at all, but quite perceptive in accurately taking the measure of my heart.

Nor did I say these things to him when I saw him, which was a chance meeting. He was in the hall when I came out of Jeff's room.

"I trust you received my note," he said. I knew it would hurt me to discourage his hopeful attitude, but I must dash those hopes.

"Yes and your apologies are accepted," I said coolly, avoiding his gaze.

The silence that followed must have been as painful for him as it was for me. Finally, he asked, "Is there nothing more to be said?"

"Nothing, except...." his eyes brightened but I quickly added, "I would like to make a trip into town to pick up a few things. Is there anyone who could drive me?"

"Of course. What time would you like to go?" His voice was as crisp and businesslike as mine had been.

"Any time this afternoon will do perfectly well. Mr. Linton usually sleeps after lunch. Perhaps that would be best."

"The car will be at the door. Shall we say one?"

"One it is." I went past him into the haven of my room.

I expected to find one of the servants waiting with a car when I came out at one. To my surprise it was David himself who stood at the open door.

"If this is intended to be some sort of joke, I find it quite unamusing," I said.

"It isn't a joke. I have some errands of my own and as we both need to go to town I see no reason at all why we shouldn't go together. Unless of course you object to my presence. I assure you I'll try not to be objectionable."

We spoke almost not all on the trip into town. There were many things I would like to have said but they remained unspoken and he remained silent and cool.

"Where would you like to go?" he asked as we started down the town's main street.

"A drugstore to begin with," I said, "but actually I'd enjoy a little window shopping. Why don't you drop me along here and I'll just ramble for an hour or so."

He pulled to the curb. "Will an hour be enough time?"

"I believe so. I'll meet you," I paused for a minute thinking, "at the train station. I know where that is."

Elsinore was a charming little town, rather old-worldish, and by the time I had made my purchases, just a few odds and ends I had run short of, I was in a much better frame of mind. I found the local people friendly. It was a small town and most of them knew already who I was. Many of them were curious but polite enough not to ask too many questions.

"You'll be the girl from up the big house," an old gentleman in the pharmacy said as he wrapped my purchases. I owned that I was.

"We hear the Mister took awfully bad a bit ago and that it was only your skill that saved him."

"Heavens," I exclaimed, laughing in embarrassment, "it was nothing more than a little elementary first aid." Mrs. Evans, one assumed, kept the town well informed of goings-on at the house. I would want to bear this in mind. In the city one could do almost what one wished without a fear that anyone two doors away would know about it. Here, every move I made in the house would soon after be known in town, and vice versa.

On my way to the train station, I passed a combination hardware and sporting goods store, and my eye was caught by a pair of ice skates in the window. I paused, remembering the little pond in the woods. I did have some time to myself each afternoon.

I purchased an inexpensive pair of skates. What with one or two other impulse purchases, and the skates dangling over my arm, I really looked quite loaded down as I set out again to the station. Almost there, I passed the coffee shop at which I had stopped on my second visit. The room beyond the glass windows looked warm and inviting. I still had a few minutes before my hour was up. I went in, taking a seat at the table where I had sat before.

The same plump little waitress came to wait on me. She remembered me too. "Afternoon," she greeted me, beaming with good-natured welcome. "Nice to see you again. How are things up at the house?"

"Quite well, thank you. Just coffee, please. Black."

She went and returned with the coffee. She still eyed me with curiosity, although by this time she knew who I was.

"You're from the city, aren't you?" she asked.

"Yes. It's quite different here."

"I'll bet." She was plainly in the mood to chat. "How are you getting along with the Mrs.?"

"Mrs. Linton, you mean? She's a very charming lady."

The smile turned mischievous. "She doesn't always take to having pretty girls around the place, if you know what I mean."

"That may explain why she hired me."

"I didn't hear that she did," she said, looking shrewd as well as mischievous. "I heard it was the Mister as hired you."

I shrugged, sorry now that I had encouraged this gossip. "It's pretty much the same thing, isn't it?"

"Not as I hear it," she insisted, not to be put off the scent that easily. "I heard there was a terrific row, him wanting to hire you, and her against it." She paused to see what I would say to this. I held my tongue.

"Looks as he won," she prodded me again.

"Or perhaps when she saw my qualifications, she decided I was suited to the job." I gathered my packages together to leave.

"You didn't finish your coffee."

"I'm late. It's been pleasant seeing you again." I hurried toward the door, eager to escape before she could get any more hooks in.

"Come back any time," she called after me, and added unnecessarily, "I love a nice chat."

I should have realized, of course, that Jeff would not have persuaded his wife to hire me without a fight. How he had finally persuaded her I didn't know, although if I talked to enough people around town, I could probably find out. No wonder I was such an object of interest to them, being as it were the center of their juiciest gossip in heaven alone knew how long.

It also put a different light on things up at the house. The waitress hadn't said so in so many words, but she had managed to convey the town's impression of a romantic triangle. It would certainly bear on anything but I did or tried to do in Jeff's behalf.

I had gone into the shop in a lighthearted mood. Now as I hurried along for the train station, I felt a growing sense of uneasiness.

It turned into genuine fear when I rounded the corner of the station and saw David. He was talking to someone and I recognized his companion as the taxi driver who had taken me up to the house on each of my visits. Nor was there any way that I could avoid an encounter, for the old man glanced up just then and saw me.

"Here she is now," he said. "Afternoon, Miss, nice to see you again."

"Good afternoon." I hurried past him with only a quick smile and a nod and opened the car door without waiting for David.

I was not quick enough, however. As David came around to the driver's side, the old man said, "Three times to the house I took her. We was becoming like old friends, just about. But I guess you won't be needing me to take you up anymore, will you, Miss?"

"One never knows. May we go along now," I said to David. "I'm afraid I've gotten a headache."

"Sure." He started up the engine. We said goodbye to the taxi driver who was still grinning and talking, more to himself than to us. Then we were on our way.

Once or twice I glanced in David's direction. He was silent and his face expressionless. I could not tell if he had grasped the significance of the man's chance remarks. I could only hope he had not.

I leaned my head back and closed my eyes. How much longer? A few days? Could I continue this charade so long?

And yet I must.

CHAPTER SIXTEEN

By the following day Jeff had pretty well recovered from his near brush with death. He was still confined to bed and too weak to be up, but his color was back. He could sit up, talk and read. I began to hope that in another day or two he would be able to get out of bed and begin moving about. Once that hurdle was crossed, we would shortly afterward be able to make our escape.

He joked about the latest poisoning, but beneath his humor was the stark and grim reality that he lived each moment in danger of his life.

"If you're going skating," he said when I told him about my purchase, "would you try not to take any falls so that you have to be put to bed again?"

"I'll try, but asking me to skate without falling is asking a lot."

Despite our joking, I had an impression that he wanted to be certain I remembered that his latest bout was my responsibility. I needed no reminding.

When I told him about the taxi driver's remarks, he frowned thoughtfully.

"I don't think David realized the significance, but I thought I ought to mention it to you."

"Yes, of course. We ought to be prepared, just in case. Let's have a story ready for them." He thought a minute more.

"How's this? I sent for you to come up. I thought you would be right for the job, and I was afraid you wouldn't take it at the price my wife was willing to pay. So I offered to supplement the figure, on the sly, so to speak."

"It makes us sound off awfully conniving," I said despondently. I was not good at concealing the truth. To have to tell such a story as this would be doubly hard.

"It's the best I can think of." He shrugged as if he could not see anything remiss in the story he wanted to tell.

"I hear you and Mary quarreled over hiring me?"

"Where did you hear that?"

"Most of the town of Elsinore knows about it, from what I could gather."

He nodded his head ruefully. "Yes, that's just one of the many disadvantages of living in the place like this. God, how I'll welcome getting out of here."

He said it with such passion I could not help drawing back a little. I could not imagine his having stayed so long with his wife, and at Elsinore, if he were as unhappy as all that. Of course, there was Mary's money.

But, I thought, he had been planning to give all that up. Hadn't he told me he had informed his wife he was going to leave—or only that he hadn't loved her?

"Are we agreed on the story we'll tell?" he interrupted my thoughts.

"Yes, I suppose so." We would have to say something if the matter came up, and I could think of no more plausible explanation.

It was as well that we had this discussion. The following day, Mary Linton, having returned from town, summoned me to her study.

When I came into the room, puzzled by the summons, I saw that David was there. He avoided my glance, turning his head away. She did not, however, and I saw that once that she was quite angry.

"Something most unpleasant as come to my attention," she began curtly. "Tell me, Miss Channing, how many times did you come to Morgan House before this last time when you came here to begin your new job?"

"Why, I...," I stammered. I found myself looking instinctively toward David but there was no comfort there. He watched me intently now but his look was a cold angry one.

"It will do you no good to lie to me," she said, "a chance remark that my brother overheard has led us to look into the matter. I should like, however, to hear from you. Did you call on this house between the time I interviewed you with my husband and the time you were actually hired?"

"Yes," I said simply. I would not cower before her, no matter what she thought of me. At the most, she could accuse me, quite wrongly, of an affair with her husband.

"So," she said with a triumphant look, "you admit to it. Now suppose you tell me why?"

"Because your husband wrote me and asked me to come."

That answer gave her pause. She waited, as if expecting something more. When it was not forthcoming, she said sharply, "well?"

"I assume," I said, my own temper rising, "that you expect me to tell you why he sent for me. I could quite frankly suggest that you ask him that. However, since he is ill and I am responsible for his health, I shall spare him as much excitement as possible and give you the answer to that myself.

"Your husband asked me to come to see him again. He made it seem urgent. When I came, you were not here. He said that he wanted me for the job, and that my qualifications particularly impressed him. He thought rightly that I would be interested in the job only if the compensation were little more. However, he said you did not want to hire me and that having persuaded you to his way of thinking, he did not want to suggest that you offer me a higher pay to interest me in the job. So, quite simply, he offered to make up the difference between what you were willing to pay and what I wanted."

"I'm sure you know," Mary said, "that I cannot permit you to remain here after this. I shall see that you are given adequate separation pay and recompensed for your travels, all of them. I shall expect you to leave immediately."

My heart jumped. I did not mind if she insulted me or was rude to me, but if she sent me away, she defeated my entire purpose for being here. "I'm afraid," I said boldly, "that I cannot accept that dismissal unless it comes from Mr. Linton."

Neither of them had expected this sort of defiance. Her eyes went wide, and her mouth literally fell open.

As for David, I had the feeling, although I might only have imagined it, that he found this turn of events amusing. He went to stand by the window, his back to us.

Mary was so taken aback that she could not speak of all for several moments. When at last she regained her voice, it was to say, "very well, you shall hear it from my husband. Come with me."

She almost flew from the room, her full sport skirt billowing behind are as she went. I hurried after her.

She was already in Jeff's room by the time I came up the stairs. Their voices could be heard even out here in the hall.

"I tell you I won't have her here," Mary screamed. "She goes today."

"And just what's to happen to me?" Jeff demanded in a voice no softer or gentler than hers. "I almost died the other night, and I would have if it hadn't been for her. I tell you, if Miss Channing leaves, I'm leaving. I'll go into New York, to Dr. Dorian. He has a nice little clinic out in Phoenix."

"I can't go to Phoenix just now, you know that...."

"Not you, me! I can and will go. I'm not going to die in this stinking bed because you're jealous of someone younger and prettier than you are!"

There was a profound silence after this. Thinking that I had really heard too much, I backed away in the direction of my own room.

Something else was said in a greatly lowered voice, I couldn't hear the words. Suddenly Mary came out of his room, throwing the door open with such force that it crashed back against the wall. Her face was wild with fury, her eyes flashing.

She saw me and stopped. I thought for a moment she meant to pounce on me like some enraged jungle cat.

"All I want from you," she said in an icy voice, "is one mistake. Just one."

She went by me and down the stairs, leaving me to stand shaken and trembling. If there had been danger in this house before it had multiplied a hundredfold now.

CHAPTER SEVENTEEN

Mary Linton's open resentment and David's coolness, gave me a good excuse to eat dinner in my own room. This time no one came to persuade me otherwise.

As for Jeff, he was recovering rapidly. The day after his violent quarrel with his wife, he was able to get out of bed and move about his room. I began to think of leaving Morgan House. It could not be long now.

"Soon," he said, echoing my thoughts. "A few more days. I know you're getting impatient, Chris and I'm trying to hurry it along."

"Don't push things. It'll only delay us if you overdo it and have a setback."

"Don't worry," he said confidently, "we've got them beaten now."

During the afternoon, with Jeff safely resting and David no longer pursuing my company, I had several hours in which to entertain myself. I took the first opportunity to carry my skates with me and set out to the pond in the woods.

We were well into winter now. Another snow had fallen during the night, a light one, but this time the ground was cold enough that the snow stayed, and now the starkness of the land was softened by fluffy drifts of snow. The branches of the trees wore little antimacassars of the same white fleece. The surface of the pond was like pewter, smooth and gleaming as if lighted from underneath.

I sat on an old log at the edge of the pond and fastened on the skates and in a few minutes I was gliding across the ice. It was a far cry from Rockefeller plaza, but in this storybook setting it would have been impossible to remain depressed, and I felt my spirits lifting.

I was no Peggy Fleming, but I considered myself competent. I had even mastered a few simple turns and a spin, although my heavy, long coat made that a little awkward. I had the place to myself, however, with no one to see if I made a mistake or fell, which I did once, landing heavily on the hard ice. Nothing was hurt but my dignity and when I saw a large black bird in a tree eyeing me with some curiosity, I laughed aloud and scrambled to my feet, brushing off the back of my coat.

As it turned out, I did not entirely have the place to myself. I was still brushing the snow off my coat, when a voice said, "You didn't hurt yourself, did you?"

I jumped, almost landing on the ice again and turned around. Where the young man had come from, I had no idea. I would have sworn there had been no one on the bank of the pond a moment before, and yet there he was, as if he had just materialized from the snow itself.

I thought at once of Hawthorne's Childish Miracle. Here was certainly the brother of the little snow-image. His face under the cap he wore was just as white, with the pale pink tint to the cheeks, and there the golden curls spilling from beneath the cap. He was dressed in white, a fur trimmed coat. He really might have been a snowdrift come to life.

"No," I replied, "but have you ever wanted to crawl under the ice?"

He laughed. He did indeed glisten with the frosty brightness of an icicle. I wondered fancifully if he would melt away should he got too near a fire. I skated in his direction.

"Am I taking your place? I didn't know anyone else came here."

I had been looking toward the sun when I first saw him, its oblique rays partially blinding me. Coming closer, the fanciful illusion faded a bit. He wasn't really all in white, although his coat was trimmed with white fur of some sort. For the rest, he had been climbing about in some deep snow and quite a bit of it still clung him. That accounted for some of the bright sparkle, too. As he moved, the snowflakes clinging to him glinted in the afternoon sun.

But he had quite enough sparkle of his own, even at close range. His youthful face looked to have been fashioned of that heavenly white and pink marble that the Italian masters were so fond of. His eyes were appropriately blue and crystalline, like ice, the equal of any frost in their sparkle. And his smile came often and brightly.

"I don't come to skate. Not as a rule, anyway."

"What a pity. I was just thinking it would be pleasant to have some company. I suppose living near this you could put me to shame."

"Well, I could show you how to get that spin right," he said with disarming frankness.

"So much for my chances at an Olympic medal," I said with a laugh. "All right, so I'm a mediocre skater. I'm Chris Channing, by the way."

"I know," he said, giving me a gloved hand. "I'm Peter Evans."

I thought for a moment. "Not Mrs. Evans' son?"

"I'd have to be some Mrs. Evans' son, wouldn't I?" he asked, teasing. "But I'm Mrs. Evans'—your Mrs. Evans, up at the house—grandson."

"Which is how you knew who I am." I was getting used to the idea that I was a good source of local gossip

"I didn't know you skated, though."

"I just picked up the skates in town. And I really would enjoy some company, if you want to bring your skates someday. By the way, if it's not too personal, since you aren't here to skate, what are you here for?"

"Trapping."

"Trapping?"

"Animals." He had a bag slung over one shoulder and he held

the open for my inspection. "See?"

"Ugh," I said with a grimace, turning away from the sight of the limp creatures inside.

"Muskrats, mostly," he said, taking no offense. This was, I suppose, a part of life here. "Caught a weasel a few days ago and a fox last week. They're pests, you know." He said this in the way of justifying what I obviously did not approve of.

I noticed he was also carrying a metal contraption that had been hidden by the bag. It was steel, consisting of some bent bars with ragged looking teeth and a spring, all of it attached to links of chain.

"I suppose that's one of the traps."

"Um-uum. It got bent, so I'm taking it home to straighten it out."

"I hope these things aren't anywhere where I'm likely to step on them," I said, eyeing it a bit uneasily. "It looks like it could take the leg right off."

"It could play the devil with your foot. But don't worry, you'd have to be really climbing around in the brush to get into one. I put them where the animals travel, which is where they're sure people won't."

"I'll remember that if I'm ever tempted to go climbing around in the bushes."

"Well, I've got to be going." he slung his bag of dead animals over his shoulder. "Maybe I will bring my skates along one of these days."

"Fine. And you'll help me with that spin?"

He nodded "Oh, by the way, I don't know if anybody thought to warn you about this ice. The water is pretty quick running underneath, so the ice thaws fast."

I gave the surface of the pond a doubtful look. "It seems solid enough."

"It'll be all right today. But if the weather should warm up it'll thaw in a hurry."

He left, pausing at the crest of the hill to wave again. Then he was gone, disappearing into the snowy scene with the same elusive impression that he was really only a part of it, a creature of the snow and frost.

It was time I should the back at the house. "One spill is enough for the day anyway," I said aloud. I sat back down on my log to remove the skates, rubbing my ankles. It had been a while since I had done any skating.

On my way back to the house I watched to see if I could spy any of my young snow-images traps. I saw nothing, of course, but he had told me that he placed them where the animals were likely to travel, and presumably no self-respecting muskrat would use the path I was on. And what was a muskrat, anyway? It sounded particularly odious.

Besides, if weasels and foxes, who were known to be shrewd, could not spot his traps, there was little likelihood that a city-bred creature like myself would see them, wherever they were.

And just as well. At the moment, I did not need to be reminded of death.

CHAPTER EIGHTEEN

To my surprise, Mrs. Evans greeted me with, "Some mail came for you, Miss. I put it in your room."

Only one person knew where I was. Before leaving, I had given Jerry this address and a key to my apartment, so that he could look in on that from time to time.

"Oh, by the way," I said as I started from the kitchen, "I met your grandson in the woods today. He's quite a charming young man."

She beamed with grandmotherly pride. I did not need to be told that he was the apple of her eye. "A fine young man, I like to think," she said. "He'll be sixteen next month. Seems like only yesterday I was babysitting with him as his parents went to the grange, and one of these days soon he'll be going on dates."

I thought to myself that if that young man didn't already have some young lady's eye, things had changed quite a bit from my generation to his. But I saw no need to remind her that boys become men.

"He's going to give me skating lessons," I said instead.

"Why, I thought you already knew how to skate."

"Not to his satisfaction."

She chuckled and bobbed her head knowingly. "That's him all right, a perfectionist. I hope you didn't take offense, miss. He speaks his mind, but he doesn't mean to hurt anyone's feelings. I've never known so gentle a boy when it comes to caring about other people."

"It would take a pretty thin skin to be offended by your

grandson." Of course, she was fairly pleased to hear these compliments, and when I left, she was beaming and humming a cheerful little tune.

The letter was indeed from Jerry. It was brief, and as I read it my good spirits abandoned me again.

"Sorry to have to send bad news," he wrote, "but when I checked your apartment today, I found that someone had broken into it. It didn't look as if much of anything had been taken. Your jewelry case was on the dresser and looked like it was untouched. Nothing seemed to be missing from the living room, but you'll have to check that out for yourself when you get back. It really looked as if someone was hunting for something. Can't tell if they found it or not. Well, that's it. Let me know what you want me to do, if anything. How is everything with you? Are you all right? Let me hear from you."

I sat for a moment thinking. Robberies weren't unusual anymore, not in the city and especially in an apartment whose owner has been away for a time. It was probably a routine house-breaking, someone looking for real valuables. They wouldn't have found them in my place. Any self-respecting thief would turn up his nose at my collection of junk jewelry.

Would he leave without taking anything? Why not? There actually wasn't anything there worth the taking.

And yet.... "It really looked as if someone was hunting for something...."

What might that have been, I wondered?

* * * * * * *

A day passed, and yet another. Jeff's strength was returning rapidly.

An uneasy truce had settled. Mary avoided my company as much as I avoided hers. When chance threw us together, she either ignored me or treated me with cool disdain. She made no further reference to our quarrel, and I had the idea that, seeing Jeff getting rapidly better, she was anticipating being done with me in the near future. For myself, I was certain that Jeff and I would be able to leave in no more than a week, and I wanted to do nothing to disturb the relative peace.

Peter kept his word to come and help me work on my skating. He was there the following day and was every bit as good on skates as I had guessed he would be. His slender body moved across the ice with all the power and grace that youth could muster, and I felt clumsy indeed on the ice with him.

But if he was frank in admitting I was a bit clumsy, he was also patient in helping me improve. He was a good instructor, astonishingly good for his years, and after an hour on the ice together, I really felt I had learned quite a bit.

"Well," I asked when he was helping me off with my skates, "do you think there is any hope?"

"You didn't fall down," he said, neatly sidestepping the question. But when he looked up from under the golden curls he was grinning. I lifted a foot and gave him a shove back into the snow.

"Cad. I hope at least you treat your regular girlfriend with a little more sympathy."

He blushed faintly. "Ah-hah," I said, "then I was right, there is one, isn't there?"

He turned shy of a sudden. "Not exactly," he said with a shrug.

"Meaning, your parents think you're both too young?"

He looked at me as if I had just performed some telepathic feat instead of guessing the obvious.

"Yes. Until we're sixteen anyway."

"I know your birthday is not far off. What about hers?"

"Three months almost." This delivered in a tone of voice suited to pronouncements of doom.

"Cheer up." I stood and gave my skirt a brush. "If it is the real thing, it'll pass the test of a few months' time. And if it's not...." I spread my hands.

"I guess you're right." He brightened a little. I doubted anything would perturb this young woods-sprite for long.

"How's the trapping going?" I asked, thinking to divert him from his unhappy love life.

"Not bad. Except I lost one of my traps."

"Is that usual?"

"Not really," he said seriously. "It must've been something pretty big to pull it loose. I fasten them down with wooden stakes. Maybe a fox, a big one, but I kind of doubt it. I've been afraid maybe somebody's dog got into it but nobody's said anything."

"Well, he'd be conspicuous dragging one of those wicked contraptions around. Maybe you just forgot where you put one?"

He wrinkled his nose to indicate what he thought of that suggestion.

"I'm sure it will turn up," I said, putting my skates over my shoulder. "See you tomorrow?"

"Maybe. I have some work to get caught up on, so if I make it, it'll be late, but I'll try."

* * * * * * *

I would never have dreamed I would be the one to find Peter's missing trap. He had said he put them where animals went, and not where people went, but this one was certainly where people—where I, at any rate—went.

It was at a bend in the path, where one had either to step off the path or lean to the side to keep from getting tangled in the thicket. I leaned but my scarf did not. Some errant breeze sent it into the brambles, and it caught, with me in mid-step.

It also saved my foot.

Off balance as I was, I put my foot down with no weight on it. So when the trap, invisible under a drift of old leaves and twigs, snapped shut, it only grazed my foot. It was enough, even at that, to tear the thick leather of my shoe and to bring blood, but it was not enough, as it surely would have been otherwise, to break the bones and my foot.

I jumped so violently that I landed in the bramble bush, and it took a minute to extricate myself, tearing my coat in the bargain.

I stood trembling and staring down at the black metal on the ground. I had nearly lost a foot, or least the use of one for quite some time. The crimson blood dripped onto a patch of white snow. Overhead a snowbird swooped and sang.

CHAPTER NINETEEN

My foot was hardly hurt at all, though it bled enough to look messy. It did look a bit conspicuous, and as luck would have it, David Morgan was in the kitchen conferring with Mrs. Evans about something when I let myself in.

"What the...?" He stared down at my torn shoe and bloodied foot. "Are you hurt?"

"Not badly," I said, shaking my foot as if to demonstrate that it was quite operable. "I had a narrow scrape though. I almost stepped into a trap."

"A trap?"

Mary, coming in at the same moment and seeing my foot, echoed him. "A trap—oh, what happened?"

"I nearly put my foot into an animal trap," I said again.

Mrs. Evans' hand flew to her breast. "Oh," she gasped, "not—not one of Peters?"

I bit my lip. "I'm afraid it might be."

"Your grandson's?" David asked. Mrs. Evans nodded.

"I don't understand a word of this," Mary Linton said sharply. "What kind of trap? Will someone please explain?"

Since she looked at me, and since I was after all the center of all this commotion, I tried to explain. "Steel traps, set out to catch animals. Mrs. Evans' grandson sets them out in the woods."

"How utterly horrible." Mary said, not in sympathy with my hurt foot, but in shock at hearing such devices existed. "Those poor creatures, how they must suffer. David, this must be stopped at once."

"It's not unusual," he said, "and it gets rid of pests, Mary."

"It's too ghastly, and I insist it be stopped."

"He'll be so unhappy," I said.

"I'm afraid it's not just about the animals," David said, "this in is an example of dangerous negligence. You might have been seriously hurt. The next person may not be so lucky."

"I insist he be ordered to stop setting those things at once," Mary said. Having delivered her ultimatum, she swept from the room.

"I'm afraid you'd better have Peter come and see me," David told the housekeeper. "I won't rave and rant at him. I'll put it on the man-to-man basis."

She seemed a bit mollified and went off to use the telephone. He said to me, "You'd better have someone look at that."

"It's only a surface cut, really. It hardly even hurts."

"Those things are never too clean, though. There's always a danger of tetanus. Better let me drive you into Dr. Mallory, unless you have something here?"

"Tetanus injection? No, and I suppose you're right, it would be wise to have one." He did not seem to notice that it had been he giving me, supposedly a nurse, medical advice.

On the drive into town, I broached the subject of David's upcoming interview with Peter. "Even granting that he was awfully careless," I said, "oughtn't a reprimand be enough? I'm sure he wouldn't let it happen a second time."

"And if he did?"

"Oh, that's being unduly harsh, isn't it? He does not impress me as a willy-nilly type of boy. He's intelligent and polite, and I'm certain he's going to be hurt over this far more than I was."

"That may be, but letting him off just like that isn't going to do his character much good, is it?"

"I think his character is basically sound."

He glanced in my direction, "But you're the one who almost lost a few toes in that contraption. Doesn't his carelessness frighten you a little?"

"Oh, I'm frightened," I said, which was not quite a direct answer to his question. "But I can't see that bearing down heavily on that young man is going to accomplish anything except making him unhappy. David you could intercede with Mary. If you talk to her, she'll surely relent. Even if he's restricted to just part of the land...."

"We'll see," he said, in a voice that said the discussion was ended for now. I let it drop, afraid that to push it further might just set him against me.

Dr. Mallory examined the cut, which was surprisingly small for the amount of blood and confusion it had caused. He washed and dressed it, and gave me a tetanus injection.

David and I spoke little on the way home. I felt it best to let him think things over for himself.

At home, despite David's insistence I should go to bed, I gave my attention to Jeff's dinner.

"I could take care of that," Mrs. Evans said.

"It's all right. To tell the truth, I'm afraid that if I miss my duties again as a result of another accident, the Lintons might decide I'm not too reliable as a nurse, and replace me with someone less accident-prone."

I was sure she knew of the argument between Jeff and Mary over keeping me on, and I thought this explanation would fit in well with that. I did not want to hurt her feelings by rejecting her offer and insisting on taking care of Jeff myself, but I did not want to forgo my responsibility either.

Jeff was up, reading, when I came into his room "I hear you had another bit of excitement," he said, putting aside his book. "I was half afraid I might be on my own again."

"No, it wasn't that serious. At least, the actual damage wasn't, regardless of what was intended."

He gave me a puzzled look. "You think someone intended much worse to happen?"

"I don't know," I said frankly. "Were you up and around this afternoon?"

"Briefly."

"Was everyone close to the house, or did you notice that someone was out?"

"Everyone was out," he said after a moment's thought. "David went in one direction, to see a neighbor about next year's planting or something like that. Mary went into town. The cook and the serving girl had the afternoon off. And Mrs. Evans...let me see...she was working up in the attic, sorting some things out to go to the church bazaar."

"So anyone could've gone into the woods."

"Yes. And of course I was only downstairs for a short time, so I wouldn't have been likely to notice who came or went from that direction."

I sighed. "Well, for all I really can prove, it was an accident. You're looking much better today. You have a high color. In another day or two...?"

"This is Tuesday,." He glanced at the calendar on the wall. "Let's mark Friday in our minds as D-day, depending, on how things go in the meantime."

I was in my room somewhat later when a knock came at the door. I was surprised to find Peter Evans there, looking despondent. I thought again of the snow-image and Hawthorne's tale. Whereas before Peter had been brilliant and gleaming, he looked now as dull and drooping as a thaw.

"Peter," I said, opening the door wide, "this is a surprise, come in." He came dispiritedly into the room. I had finished my dinner a short time before, but there was still a thermos of hot coffee on the tray.

"Would you like some coffee?" I asked.

"No, thank you." He turned his hat about in his hands and studied the floor. "My mom and dad said I had to make a special point of coming and apologizing to you for what happened."

"It's quite all right, Peter. We'll talk about that in a minute. But first, tell me, did Mr. Morgan say it would be all right to continue your trapping?"

He nodded. "Just in the far field. He said he wouldn't allow even that, but I had you to thank. So, thanks."

He did look up then, and his handsome, open face was frankly puzzled. "Honestly, Miss Chris, I don't know how that trap got where it was. I never put them where people could step on them."

"I know." I put a finger to my lips and went to close the door. Then, in a lowered voice, I said, "you mustn't blame yourself for what happened, Peter. It wasn't your fault. That wasn't where you had put the trap. You see, I checked, and there was no stake holding it in place there."

He breathed a deep sigh of relief. "Boy, am I happy to hear that. Then some animal must of dragged it...." he came to a stop. His keen young mind saw in a flash what it had taken me several hours to grasp.

"But if some animal got caught in it and dragged it there," he said, looking puzzled again, "it would already have been sprung."

I put a hand on his shoulder. "Peter, I'm going to ask a big favor of you, please. Don't say anything more about this to anyone."

"They'll go on thinking it was because I was careless."

"I know. It's asking a lot of you on such short acquaintance. All I can say is that it's very important to me."

He only needed a moment to consider the request. "Whatever you say," he said with a grin and a shrug.

"Good. I promise you I'll see everyone gets the real story in due time."

He went to the door and paused in the act of turning the knob. "You know, if you need any help or anything, you can call on me."

He gave the words a weight beyond their simple meaning. In that moment, I thought he looked very grown up and manly, and a wave of affection and gratitude went through me.

"I may find that I need a man on my side. If I do you'll be the first one I call."

We left it at that, but we understood, each of us, what the other had been saying without putting it in so many words. He had understood that the incident with his lost trap had some significance beyond what I had told him. No animal had dragged it to where it was, then reset it and hid it so it could not be seen. And he certainly had not set it where it was. And understanding all this, he had grasped that I might be in some sort of trouble or danger and had offered his protection.

Well, my fine young man, I thought, before all this is settled, I just might need it. And I hope you're as strong and as capable as you look.

CHAPTER TWENTY

I went the following day to the spot where the trap had been set. What exactly I expected to find I had no idea, and I found nothing. The trap was gone from where I had put it aside in the bushes, but probably Peter had fetched it. In any event, there was nothing to be seen but some spots of dried blood on the ground, barely distinguishable.

I suppose I thought I might find some clue as to how the trap had come to be where it was, but if any such clues remained, they did not appear to my amateur's eye.

Having brought my skates, I went on to the pond. I was careful to watch my step today, even in the most open stretches of the path. I didn't really expect lightning to strike in the same place twice, but I was taking no chances.

It was quite a bit warmer this day, one of those abrupt changes of weather which occur even in the heart of winter. Most of the snow, and there had been only scattered patches and drifts, had melted in the winter sunlight, but the pond still gleamed with its covering of ice.

I was sorry that Peter was not here, but David's decision on the trapping had banished him to the field beyond this one, so I suppose I would not be encountering him on these strolls in the woods.

So far as that goes, I told myself, strapping on the skates, there were not going to be so many strolls in the future. This was Wednesday and all indications were Jeff would be well enough to leave the house on Friday. He was up again today, dressed even and he had felt so well that he balked at going to bed to rest after lunch and had to be argued into it.

We had even gone so far as to make plans for our departure, talking in whispers when I went to take him his bedtime milk. We planned on Friday morning. We would go into town to pay a visit to the good Dr. Mallory, our excuse that there were a few questions I wanted the doctor's advice on, and Jeff would supply the additional motive, if it was needed, that he simply was suffering cabin fever and wanted to get out of the house for a spell.

The difficult part would be assuring that we made the trip unchaperoned. Mary might very well insist on coming with us, or she might be afraid that Jeff was not able to drive the car. It was necessary that Jeff seemed quite well enough to manage the driving.

With this in mind it was important that he be seen up and around, having the freedom of the house as much as possible during the intervening period, to dispel any impressions of clinging weakness. We would have trouble enough escaping Mary's jealous eye without that additional difficulty.

"And that," I had told Jeff a short time before, sending him firmly to bed, "is why you need your rest, so there's no danger of a setback."

At the very least, I was certain we would be able to manage a departure on Saturday.

Once we got to Elsinore, we would head straight for the train station, timing our arrival to get us there just a few minutes before the train left for New York City. Somehow (we had not quite worked out this detail to my satisfaction) we would have gotten our luggage into the trunk of the car before leaving the house.

"Leave that to me," Jeff insisted. "If worse comes to worst, we can just leave everything behind. I don't care if I have to go with nothing more than the clothes on my back."

So, despite the ominous accident with the trap my spirits were up, and I took to the ice with the sense of exhilaration.

I practiced the spin Peter taught me to do, again wishing he were here with me. I did not fall this time and did it again just for good measure. Because I was pleased with myself and because it seemed that this unpleasant interlude in my life would soon be over, and because the sun was golden and almost tangible about me, I threw back my head and laughed aloud. I turned, gliding backward.

As I looked up, I saw David. He was standing at the bluff across the pond, feet planted widely and firmly, looking tall and powerful and incredibly handsome. My breath caught in my throat.

I waved at him and turned back toward the center of the ice. I had heard a sound just as I saw David standing above me, a creaking sound, not unlike the creaking of floorboards in an old house. I was accustomed to rink-skating and so I did not grasp the full significance of the sound until I suddenly felt the ice beneath my feet move slightly. From somewhere below and off to the right came a loud report, like the breaking of a piece of glass.

I knew in a horrible flash of insight what was happening. The weather had turned warmer. True to Peter's warning, the ice had begun to melt.

Now it was breaking beneath me!

CHAPTER TWENTY-ONE

It must have taken a second or two, no longer, for me to plunge into the icy water, yet it seemed as if it took hours, as if it happened in slow motion.

That eerie parting of the ice beneath me, the futile, hopeless attempt to skate faster than the ice could break, to leap to safety—then I was crashing through and down, jagged edges of ice cutting at my arms and legs.

The darkness of the water, so cold it literally took the breath away, closed over me. I hit bottom, the tentacles of some underwater plant tickling my legs. I coughed and choked, swallowing water instead of air. My lungs hurt as I fought the blackness wildly, arching upward, to crash against a hard surface where I expected air.

I was under the ice!

Panic made me helpless. My eyes opened, staring of the opaque light above, hitting the solid surface. But the same ice that had been too flimsy to support my weight was too strong to be knocked aside from beneath. My arms flailed out, my legs thrashed. I was trapped here in an icy, watery grave.

I fought down the panic. One of the skates slipped off, and even that loss seemed to help. My clothes were like an anchor, trying to hold me down—coat, dress, scarf, shoes—all soaked now with water. And the cold coursing through my veins numbed me, until my limbs felt as if they could not be moved, as if they were frozen into solid blocks of ice.

Ice. Solid, immovable ice. It was as if the covering of the pond had opened up just long enough to swallow me and had closed again over itself, sealing me in this dark, numbing tomb. My chest felt as if the torch were searing it from the inside, while I froze from the outside. My lungs were bursting, bursting....

I found the opening at last, feeling along the sheet of ice above me, my hands suddenly plunging upward into the air. I grabbed the edge, throwing myself upward, gasping for air, coughing.

The ice broke in my hands, and again I sank downward, the water closing above me. This time, though, I did not touch bottom nor drift away from the opening, and I bobbed up into the sunlight again.

David, I thought with a sense of relief. David was here, and in a matter of seconds he would come to rescue me from this icy grave.

As I bobbed to the surface, clutching at the jagged edges of the ice, my eyes went to the bluff where he been standing.

He was gone!

The ice broke again, unable to hold my clinging weight, and I sank, swallowing still more water. My forehead struck one of the sharp edges, but I scarcely felt the pain, and only dimly perceived the reddening of the water about me. My hands were scarcely functioning, only just able to claw at the ice. The weight of my sodden clothes dragged me down.

He couldn't have gone, my frantic mind cried, not seeing me like this. It wasn't possible that he could go and leave me to drown in this awful way, too weak now even to think of climbing onto the ice, even if the ice would hold me.

"Chris! Chris, hold on!"

I thought at first it was David after all, but it wasn't, I realized a second later. It had been a young voice, a boy's voice.

A moment later, as I willed my feet to move, to tread water, while I held with nearly paralyzed fingers to a pointing fragment of ice, I saw Peter racing to the edge of the pond.

"Hang on," he yelled.

He dropped to the ground and slid onto the ice on his belly. I knew what he was doing. His weight was distributed over a greater area this way, lessening the danger of the ice breaking beneath him also. It seemed an eternity that I watched and waited as he inched his way out.

The ice creaked and swayed. He put his hand as far as he could and I reached for it, stretching as if I could stand on tiptoe in the water.

Our hands were almost a foot apart.

"It's no use," I sobbed, slipping down again into the water.

"Wait." He turned on his side and began to undo the buckle of his belt. A moment later he had tugged the belt free of his trousers.

"Here." He threw the end with the buckle to me. I caught it, holding it weakly. He doubled the other end about his hand.

"Go on," he said, "pull yourself up with it. I can hold you."

"I can't," I said, gasping. My fingers refused to obey my commands.

"You can." He said. "You've got to. Hurry."

I was holding the ice with one hand, the buckle of the belt with the other. I bit into my lip, holding my breath, and willed my hand to grip the belt above the brass buckle. For a second I thought I had lost all use of my fingers. I felt literally frozen. I scarcely felt the change when they did tighten, but my eyes told me that my grasp was firm now. I let go of the ice and seized the belt with my other hand.

I shall never be able to recall fully how I climbed from that freezing pool to the surface of the ice. I remember his coaxing me, ordering me, begging me. I remember the ice breaking again, and my horror that Peter might fall in and drown with me. I remember somehow getting a leg up onto the ice. That limb alone felt as if it weighed a ton or more.

But somehow, after what might have been hours, I was on the ice, lying flat on my stomach, gasping and retching.

"Gently," Peter was saying. "As gently as possible."

Beneath me the ice creaked and shook. I tried to inch myself along, holding to the belt. Snaking himself backwards Peter pulled and coaxed me along. He reached the thick, completely solid ice at the edge, and then he was grabbing me and pulling me to the bank. I sank into his arms.

It was several moments before either of us could get our breath back enough to move. Then it was Peter, who roused me to action.

"Here," he said, making me sit up while he took off his coat. "Put this on before you catch pneumonia."

"What about you?" I asked through chattering teeth.

"I'm not soaked to the skin like you. Better take that coat of yours off, it's only going to make you that much colder."

I gladly did as he said, putting his warm dry coat on over my wet dress. It gave me some comfort, at least, although I still felt numb with the cold. My shivering was nearly convulsive.

"We'll have to get you back to the house." He gave me a dubious look. "Can you walk if I help you?"

What he meant plainly was that he would never be able to carry me all that distance.

"There isn't much choice is there?"

"I can leave you here and go for help," he said, his tone making it clear what he thought of that idea.

"I'd be a solid block of ice by the time you got back. Help me up will you?"

I was still weak and numb but with his help I could stand and walk. We started for the house, walking slowly and unsteadily.

My body moved automatically. My mind was elsewhere. I was thinking of David, who had disappeared. Had he seen me fall into the water? Surely not, or he would have come to rescue me himself.

But he had been there just seconds before the ice broke. Had the worst possible luck removed him from the scene mere fractions of seconds too soon?

The alternative was so frightening I could not accept it. Yet, in the context of all that had occurred time since I had first come to Morgan House, I could not altogether dismiss from my mind the possibility that David had still been watching seconds after I waved at him, when I fell through the ice.

And if he had been, and had gone away without trying to save me—why, then, it could only mean he had meant for me to die.

CHAPTER TWENTY-TWO

I can scarcely describe what it cost me to drag myself, with Peter's arm supporting me as much as he was able, along that path through the woods, wearing those dripping, icy clothes. At one point I thought it inconceivable that anyone could feel so cold and yet live and move.

Eventually, we made it, pausing to lean against one of the outbuildings while I gasped weakly for breath.

"Can you make it the rest of the way?" Peter asked. He sounded only slightly less breathless than I.

"I'll make it." I summoned up a final reserve of strength from I knew not where, and forced my leaden, shivering limbs to move again. We stumbled through a forgotten heap of old leaves. I stubbed my toe on something and cried out.

The next moment, the door from the kitchen opened and Mrs. Evans came out. "Merciful heavens!" she exclaimed at the sight of us, and what a sight we must have been.

Peter said something in reply, but I only half heard it and have no idea what was. It might have been a foreign tongue, and I certainly couldn't have answered in any event. I could only stumble blindly forward toward the warmth of the house.

I reached the kitchen threshold and then I sank to my knees, the room spinning wildly and resolving itself into darkness.

It was only a brief blackout, lasting for perhaps seconds. From somewhere beyond the blackness, I heard voices, excited, frightened—Mrs. Evans' voice trying to question and scold and order about all at once. Peter's, voice, strained, trying to explain.

I was half-dragged, half-carried into the house. Somehow, David appeared on the scene, exclaiming in surprise and then taking charge.

He carried me up the stairs. I no longer needed to worry or struggle to reach safety. Details blurred. I was in my room, a fire suddenly blazing, giving much needed light and warmth.

"Peter," I stammered, remembering through the haze of exhaustion how brave and manly he had been. "He must be frozen."

"Never you mind about Peter," Mrs. Evans said, yanking at my clothes. "He'll be all right."

Together we got me out of my sopping garments. I guessed that David had been banished from the room, although I don't think I would have cared if the entire village population had been there. My brain was as numb as my body.

She pushed me into a chair before the fire, wrapped in a big thick robe.

From somewhere—I suppose other people must have been coming and going, but they were beyond the range of my awareness—Mrs. Evans produced a bowl of some sort of soup. It was hot and thick and filling, I think the most delicious thing I've ever tasted. I ate quickly, greedily, savoring the way the heat from the soup seemed to seep down through me, settled in my cold joints and thawing them.

Finally I was hustled off to bed, tucked in like a helpless child and, warmed by the fire and the soup, I slept.

* * * * * * *

"Miss Channing, Miss Channing, wake up." It was Mrs. Evans shaking me, trying to rouse me. "You're having bad dreams, dear."

I struggled upward through the darkness, managing at last to open my eyes and look into the concerned face above mine.

"You were having an awful bad dream, dear," Mrs. Evans said. "I just came up to look in on you and you were crying and thrashing about."

For a moment I lay still, trying to dispel the lingering sense of terror that my dream had inspired. But the dream itself I could not remember. The room was cold. My fire had burned out

"I expect it's that accident still preying on your mind," Mrs. Evans said. "Here, you sit up and get yourself collected and I'll stir up the fire for you. It's like a tomb in here."

I found the choice of words disconcerting. I did sit up against the headboard, wrapping the blanket close about me. She poked and prodded the fire until it was blazing again, its friendly glow bringing a sense of comfort.

"Mr. Linton," I said while she worked, "I didn't get to fix dinner for him." I recalled with a feeling of guilt what had happened the last time I was derelict in my duty.

"I did it myself."

"Quite by yourself?"

"Yes, Miss. He was upset to hear that you are sick and wouldn't be able to look after him, so I told them I would manage everything with my own two hands. That seemed to satisfy him. Of course, I told him how sick you were, and he was concerned."

I'm sure he was, I thought, but not because of any great concern for me. I knew Jeffrey too well now for that. He was afraid for himself—not without justification, as far as that went.

Well, if Mrs. Evans had taken care of his dinner herself, that ought to ensure that it was safe enough. Whatever might be going on this house, I was quite convinced the housekeeper was no part of it. She was old fashioned, no nonsense goodness personified.

"Thank you very much," I said when she had the fire burning again and was preparing to leave.

"Will you be all right now? I could fetch a cot up here and sleep nearby if that would make you feel better. Or bring you some hot tea."

"No, nothing, thank you. You've been most kind, Mrs. Evans."

As she was leaving I asked, "How is Peter?"

"Oh, he's fine, miss. You know how young people are, strong as oxes when it comes down to it. He was mostly worried about you."

"I owe him my life. He's a brave young man. You have a right to be quite proud of him."

She looked close to bursting with pride. "I've always thought he was a good boy," she said with admirable modesty. "Well, good night now, Miss. If you need anything during the night, you ring for me, never mind how late it is."

But when she had gone I did not feel like going to sleep again. I got up, donning the big robe again and sat before the fire, grateful for its penetrating warmth, thinking.

It was dawn before I again crawled into my bed and slept.

CHAPTER TWENTY-THREE

Jeff came to see me early in the morning. It gave me a feeling of relief to see that he appeared unaffected by the loss of my ministrations for one evening. Mrs. Evans had apparently kept a careful eye on things, without even knowing what it was she was guarding against.

"You seem determined to get yourself put to bed," he said in a teasing voice. I was afraid he would be petulant this morning, but he did not seem to be.

"It's been my season for accidents, hasn't it?"

"And it was only an accident?" he asked in a lowered voice.

"Yes I don't see how it could have been anything else. Peter had warned me about that ice thawing if the weather turned, but I really just forgot." I could not bring myself to tell him of my nagging suspicion that David had seen me fall through the ice and had left without attempting to rescue me. Surely that hadn't really happened.

"You look like you're pretty well recovered." I was out of bed and had just finished the warm breakfast Mrs. Evans had brought me earlier.

"Well, I have felt better in my life," I admitted with a wry grin. "But honestly, I don't feel one third as bad as I expected. Stiff and sore and a stopped-up head, but I expected a first rate case of pneumonia."

David came in just then. He paused at the open door, the two men bristling at one another like strange dogs.

"Well," Jeff said, giving me a look that David fortunately

could not see, "since it's your day to play the role of patient, I shall excuse myself and let you enjoy it."

When he had gone, David came closer. It set my heart stirring to see how anxious he looked.

"I feel as if I were partly to blame for what happened," he said. "I should've warned you about the ice."

"I had been warned. Peter mentioned it."

"It must've happened right after I left."

"Within a few seconds. One minute you were there and I was skating safely. The next, I was through the ice and you were gone."

I don't know if my voice conveyed the fear that had been haunting me but he said impetuously, "a few seconds. My god, I'd never have forgiven myself if you hadn't gotten out of there."

Then, suddenly, I was in his arms. "Chris, darling," he murmured holding me close, "I love you. I don't care if you don't love me in return. I can't change the way I feel."

"But I do love you."

"Darling." His lips found mine and we kissed.

I shut my eyes and forgot everything but that I loved him.

"Then we can go away together," he said as our lips parted. He felt me stiffen in his arms. "What's the matter?"

"I...I can't go away with you," I stammered, unable to meet his gaze. "Not now."

"But why not.? What's to keep you here, unless...." He paused, his eyes suddenly turning cold. "Unless there's someone else, someone here that you can't be parted from."

"David, I—"

He let me go so abruptly I nearly fell. "No, don't say it," he said angrily. "I think I understand."

He was gone before I could say anything more. I sank into my chair again, feeling utterly miserable. So this was love? This feeling of hopelessness, of misery and rejection? And I had somehow always thought it would be a wonderfully happy experience when it came to me again.

Later, when I had accomplished the purpose for which for I

had come here, and had seen Jeff safely in the city, I would write to David. I would tell him everything and put myself completely at his mercy.

He might hate me or think me a fool, but I would be gambling then only with my own happiness and well-being, and no one else's. Then we would see if his love was equal to that test. But until then, I could do nothing to disprove his jealous suspicions.

* * * * * * *

That same afternoon Mary Linton sent for me and asked if I would come to her study. Since she had not come to check on me after the accident, I thought perhaps she wanted to do so now, although it seemed peculiar to me that she would ask me to come to her that purpose, rather than the other way around. Since I was up, however, and feeling well for the most part, I had no reason to object.

I found both Mary and David waiting in the study. I was not surprised when David looked upon me coldly. I supposed he was still angry with me and I could not but admit that he had a right to be.

In place of the polite sympathy I had expected from Mary, however, I found cold anger. She did not even speak when I came into the room, but stood by her desk glowering at me for a full minute.

"Mrs. Evans said you wanted to see me," I said, breaking the awkward silence.

"Yes," she said curtly.

When she still continued to look at me with an expression of loathing, I said, "May I ask why?"

"I should think you would know why." A bitter smile twisted her mouth.

I felt a flash of anger. "Indeed perhaps I should, but the fact is I do not. Is there something in particular you wish to discuss with me, or am I to suppose you have simply been pining for my company?"

"Something in particular? Yes there certainly is. I should like to know how long you've been having an affair with my husband?"

That question so startled me that I must have looked the picture of guilt itself. My face went white, and for a moment I could hardly find my voice. "Why...I've been doing no such thing!" I stammered, annoyed with myself for my lack of aplomb. But of course, my presence here in the house was not entirely free of guilt. I was guilty of deception. That guilt no doubt showed plainly enough on my face.

"I say that you have. I say that you're lying."

My chin went up as my anger flared. "I think I've heard enough of this."

I would have gone then but she said, "Just a moment," in a voice that brought me to a halt.

I turned back to her. I was shocked in glancing at David to see no less loathing in his eyes than hers. He believed her accusation, of course. I could see how it fitted with his own suspicions.

"Do you take me for a fool?" she demanded. "Even if I had no proof, the truth can be seen in your very eyes. Your guilt is as obvious as the nose on your face."

"What proof could you possibly have of these ridiculous charges?"

She smiled again, this time in triumph. "The very best kind. Proof in your own words."

She seized a bundle of papers from the desk and thrust them toward me with a powerful gesture. "Here, here is my proof. Look at them."

I took the bundle from her. They were letters, tied together with a string. I turned them over. As my eyes fell on the handwriting my eyes widened and my mouth fell open.

"You do recognize them, don't you?" she asked scornfully.

"I...I don't know," I said, stalling for time while my brain sought feverishly for some explanation. Of course, I did recognize them. The handwriting was my own. I had written these letters, I knew that even before I undid the string and began to read them.

There was no real need to read them. I could probably have quoted every one of them from memory. At the time I wrote them they were charged with all of the emotion of which I had been capable.

They were the love letters I had written to Jeff.

CHAPTER TWENTY-FOUR

My hand shook as I unfolded the first of the sheets and read the words written there in a handwriting so obviously my own, for all that it had the boldness of a younger hand.

"My darling Jeff," it began, "how I wish I were a writer or a poet or an artist of some sort, so that I could more fully express the love I feel for you, so that I could tell you, in verses, in songs, on canvas, all the love that now fills me up and overflows from my heart...."

My eyes scanned the page. I felt tears threatening, tears at the heartache the foolish young girl had suffered as a result of what she the believed to be the one great love of her life. Oh, what an eternity ago it seemed, that age of nineteen!

"I cannot bear to be parted from you like this. Every day is in agony. If I could be there with you—do you think I could, darling? Perhaps we could arrange something...."

He had been away, then, on that fateful trip to Florida. I had thought I could not endure the separation.

"I can share you if I must, but I can't give you up. That is asking too much of me." My tears nearly overflowed with that one, written when I heard for the first time of Mary Morgan. There had been more to the letter than was here now. It had been a foolish letter, a tossing aside of all pride. The greatest pain had been in his ignoring it, not bothering to answer it at all, after I had thrown myself in this letter at his feet.

I forced myself to read on, despite the pain and humiliation this was costing me. They were all in the same vein, pledging my love for him, swearing that nothing must ever keep us apart, that nothing mattered to me in the entire world but him, and being with him.

All in all, they made a completely convincing record of the love I had felt for him. It was as if they had been selected exactly for that purpose. And as I read, I saw something else about them. They were on the same, plain white paper that I had always used, paper from school classes. Except, the paper had been trimmed since I had written letters on it. Trimmed exactly so that, although it looked untouched, all of the dates had been removed from the letters.

The love I had felt then was five years dead within my breast, but in these letters, signed with my name, it was as fresh, as full, as if it had lived only yesterday, or even today.

"Well," Mary said when I had looked them over.

"I...I don't know what to say." I folded the last of the letters and handed them back to her.

"You could say it wasn't true," David said, speaking for the first time since I had come into the room.

I bit my lip, looking for one to the other. How I would have liked to do what he asked. I saw the hopeful pleading in his eyes and realized with a deepening sense of despair that he wanted to believe the letters were somehow false. If I could only meet his questioning gaze and tell him that I had not written them....

I could not do it.

"Do you admit these are your letters," Mary demanded, brandishing them as if they were a weapon, which indeed they were. "Written to Jeff?"

"Chris, for god's sake," David said when I still remain silent, "say they aren't yours. Say you didn't write them."

I shook my head, biting back the tears. "I can't, David."

His shoulders drooped and the light died in his eyes. "Then it's true?" he asked softly.

"They are my letters," I admitted. "I wrote them to Jeff Linton, and I meant everything that I said in them...." Mary started to say something, but I cut her off, finishing with, "I meant it all at the time I wrote them."

"What is that supposed to mean?" she asked.

"Those letters were written five years ago. Yes, I knew Jeff then, before he had even met you. And I loved him, or I thought I did. I was only nineteen at the time. He was the first boyfriend I ever had. I spent all my teen years in finishing schools and visiting relatives. He was the first boy who ever kissed me, can you imagine how naive I was?"

It was shameful to have to bare my soul like this, while the two of them glowered. But I had to try for David's sake to make this explanation.

"The emotions expressed in those letters were expressed by that girl in the past. Believe me, she is in the past. And so is any love that I felt, or thought I felt, for Jeff. There is no affair between us. We have never so much as embraced in those five years, nor even wanted to."

I could see they did not believe this. I thought that David, at least, looked as if he wanted to believe it, but could not quite. And how could I blame him, after having deceived them for this long?

"Then how do you explain your presence here, now, in this house?" Mary asked. "Can you honestly ask me to believe that it is only coincidence?"

"I...." But I could no more ask her to believe that than I could have asked her to believe that the letters were not mine. "I think perhaps Jeff ought to be here. I think he might better answer some of these questions."

I saw David stiffen at this suggestion, but Mary seemed to welcome it. "Yes, I believe you're right," she said. She gave the bell that summoned Mrs. Evans a vicious jab with her finger. When the housekeeper did not appear at once, she rang it again angrily.

Mrs. Evans came to the door a moment later, out of breath from running to answer the impatient summons. "Yes, ma'am?" she said.

"Tell Mr. Linton we would like to see him here," Mary said.

"And if he's lying down?"

"If he's lying down, tell him to get up."

"Yes, surely." Mrs. Evans, looking shocked, disappeared into the hall.

We waited in an awkward silence. I could hardly bear to face them. I knew that we had come to some sort of crisis, and I felt as if the responsibility to carry it further ought to be Jeff's. He might very well want to put all the cards on the table, admit to his suspicions, accuse them of trying to murder him, and have it all out. But I had no right to take that step for him.

Mary Linton lit a cigarette. David only stood with his arms folded over his chest and watched me. I stared miserably down at the floor, glancing up from time to time from under my eyelashes.

It seemed an eternity later that Jeff came into the room. He wore a very smart smoking jacket. Except for his thinness and the signs of strain about the eyes and mouth he looked his old self, and quite the sophisticate.

"Well, what have we here?" he asked, strolling into the room with an attitude of nonchalance. "A gathering of the clan?"

"Nothing quite that cheerful," Mary said, thrusting the letters at him. "More a confrontation with your inamorata."

He glanced at the letters. I saw that he recognized them at once, although he took his time to look them over.

"I thought," I said, despising myself because my voice shook, "that you ought to be the one to answer Mary's questions."

"Yes," he said, nodding and giving me a wan smile. "You're right, of course. No point leaving it all on your shoulders."

I felt relieved of that, glad to have at least part of that burden lifted.

He came closer to me and put an arm about my waist. "Very well," he said, looking at David and Mary, "since the glove's already in the ring, you might as well hear it in the simplest terms possible. It's true, everything that you've guessed from those letters. Chris and I are lovers. I'm sorry, Mary, but that's the way it is."

CHAPTER TWENTY-FIVE

I was so astonished at this completely unexpected turn of events, that for a moment I could say or do nothing. I cannot even guess what my face showed. It must have registered something, because Jeff turned me toward him and said, "I'm sorry, darling. I thought it was best to have it out in the open."

I somehow managed to say, "I'd like to speak to you alone, if I may."

"It's all right, don't worry about me," David said in a venomous tone. "I think I've heard all of this that I care to hear."

He went by us and from the room without looking back once at me.

"So have I, for the moment," Mary said. Her cold gaze swept over the two of us. "This time, Jeff, I want her to leave. I don't care in the slightest what your health requires. And as for you, we will discuss the divorce proceedings when I'm feeling a little calmer."

She me, too, went out, her heels clicking along the hall outside

When we were alone, I freed myself from Jeff's embrace. "I think," I said, in a voice not much warmer than theirs had been, "that you had better give me some sort of explanation."

He shrugged and went to the table across the room, on which some decanters were sitting. He poured himself a brandy, adding a spurt of soda.

"What's to explain?" he asked. He looked altogether unconcerned.

I was furious, and his attitude was doing nothing to mitigate my anger. "How could you have said such an asinine thing?"

"Why shouldn't I have said it?"

"Because in the first place there isn't an iota of truth in it."

"Isn't there?" He cocked an eyebrow.

"No, there isn't, and you know full well there isn't."

He twirled his drink about in his glass. "What would you have had me say, my dear? That we believe they are trying to murder us and that I had imported you up here to try to save my life? Don't be a fool, Chris. I said what I did because it was the safest thing to say."

I took a deep breath and willed myself to remain calm. "The safest in what way?"

"If they think we are united, they're going to think twice about doing anything to either of us. Look at it this way. Suppose Mary did succeed in killing me. If it's out in the open that you and I are lovers, as now it is, she would be the very first person to come under suspicion. The same is true if she murdered you. By giving her such a strong motive, we've made it virtually impossible for her to do anything to us."

There was a certain logic to what he said. Still I balked at confessing to a sordid affair of which I was not guilty.

"Mary was right about one thing, at least," I said. "It is quite necessary that I leave here. I think we had better plan definitely on leaving tomorrow."

He frowned and finished off his drink. "That may be a little premature."

"I don't think so," I said firmly. "After all, there's no need now for stealing away without their knowing about it, is there? If they think we're lovers, and your wife has thrown me out, there's absolutely no reason why you shouldn't be leaving with me as quickly as possible, right?"

"I don't know...."

"Well I do," I said emphatically. "I want to leave here no later than tomorrow, Jeff. If you plan on leaving with me, you'll have to do it then. I don't wish to stay beyond tomorrow."

I went up to my own room. I was not happy with the way

events had transpired but perhaps after all it was for the best if Mary and David were convinced that Jeff and I were lovers. He was right, it might prevent them from doing anything drastic. And it gave us every reason to leave as soon as possible. Which, no matter what transpired in the meantime, I was determined to do.

In my room I thought about the scene that had just taken place downstairs. In the shock of seeing my letters, and Jeff's astonishing statement I had not thought to ask the most obvious question—where had Mary gotten my letters?

The first answer that came into my mind was that it was she who'd had my apartment searched. She had been into the city recently, but that was of no particular importance. Even had she remained here at Elsinore, she could certainly have arranged to have that done. When one had the sort of wealth she had, one was considerably less isolated from things.

But although that answer was obvious at first thought, I rejected it upon reflection. She might have had my apartment searched, but she had not found those letters there. Any letters I had received from Jeff in the past, and there had been so pitifully few of them anyway, had long since been destroyed.

The letters Mary had downstairs were the letters I had written to Jeff, not his to me. And those I certainly would not have had in my apartment.

She must have somehow gotten those letters here, from Jeff, without his knowing about it. I could not imagine what had prompted him to keep them all these years, nor through what carelessness on his part she had found them, but that was the only explanation.

The letters had certainly dealt a final blow to any hope of a romance with David. I was sure I would never manage to convince him of the truth when all of this was over. There was simply too much evidence against me when you stood outside the situation and looked at it objectively. My deception in being here, my all too obvious feelings of guilt when Mary had confronted me, my evasions with David, the letters with their damming confessions of love—even the jade pendant that I wore was a strike against me.

My hand went instinctively to my throat. The pendant was gone. I was so accustomed to wearing it that I had not even been aware of its absence. Now my throat felt strangely naked.

I stood, looking at the floor about me. It was not there, nor was it to be found in a quick search of the room. I stood by the dresser, trying to reason where it might have gone.

The answer was clear. I must have lost it in my accident on the ice the day before. Or, which was even more likely, in that stumbling, barely conscious walk back to the house afterward.

If it had come off in the water, it was gone, at least until the spring thaws made the creek bed accessible again. But if it had fallen along the path I might be able to find it. It shouldn't be too difficult to see. Much of the snow had melted, and the gold chain that held it would be shiny and easy to spot against the dry ground.

There was nothing that would satisfy my disappointment but to go looking for it. I bundled up warmly, not wanting to make my cold any worse and went back down the stairs.

Mrs. Evans was surprised to see me bundled up as I was. "Going out, Miss?" she asked.

"Yes. I lost a piece of jewelry yesterday, and I thought I might find it along the path. And, you might as well be told, since you'll know it sooner or later anyway, I'll be leaving tomorrow, Mrs. Evans."

She did not seem particularly surprised, nor did she ask if Mr. Linton was sufficiently recovered that he no longer needed my attention. I suppose she already knew of the scene that had taken place a short time ago.

"Well, we'll be missing you," she said with a genuinely friendly smile. "Peter thinks you're practically a queen, I don't mind telling you."

"I think he's rather special too. I hope I have an opportunity to say goodbye to him before I go. And I want to thank you, too, for everything you've done for me. You've been very kind."

"One doesn't mind doing for someone as appreciates it." As I was going out, she said, "be careful, Miss. You won't want to be having any more accidents."

I thanked her and set out, but her remark made me ponder. I'd had more than a reasonable share of accidents of late, and indeed I did not want to have any more. The thought made me quicken my step a little.

It was foolish to think such things, I warned myself. I wasn't going out on the ice, and I wasn't going to be in the woods long enough to run into any kind of danger. Nor was it likely that any more traps had been set along the path, although I made a point to watch my step. I was only going to be out long enough to look for my pendant.

I reached the pond without finding it, although I walked slowly and looked carefully all the way. I paused at the edge of the ice. The place where I had fallen through had not yet frozen over again. It looked frightening, yawning jaggedly opening, and I briefly relived those awful moments in the water when I had felt that my life was to end.

"Heavens," I said aloud, "there's a train of thought guaranteed to make one cheerful."

Peter had pulled me to the bank about a third of the way about the pond. I started toward that spot. I was almost there when I saw the pendant lying on the ground. The gold of the chain sparkled in the winter sunlight, catching my eye at once.

I stooped to pick it up. As I did, something rang out sharply, a cracking sound. A few feet beyond me, a patch of snow erupted in a little flurry, flakes bursting upward like a spray.

It must have been a second or two before I realized what had happened.

Someone had shot at me.

CHAPTER TWENTY-SIX

A number of thoughts flashed through my mind at once. I realized that it was my stooping down for the jade pendant that had saved my life. The bullet would have struck me had I still been standing.

The second thought was that it was some stupid hunter shooting, who had not even seen me. I reacted to this at once, crying, "Hey, watch out for me!"

I was thinking, too, that I was a sitting duck where I was, in the open with no shelter of any kind. If someone meant to shoot me....

I threw myself flat on the ground, that thought ricocheting through my brain. If they meant to shoot me, they'd certainly have no trouble doing so.

I lay clinging to the ground, frozen with fear. There was no shelter close by. The nearest was a large boulder, and it was some ten yards or so away. The trees were behind me, nearly the same distance.

Perhaps I would have been wiser to bolt for one of the other of these, but the simple truth was, I could not bring myself to get up from the ground and run for it. Instead, I lay there shivering like a frightened deer, waiting for the next shot I was sure would come any minute.

It did not come, however. Seconds dragged by, each of them seeming like an eternity, and nothing at all happened. My face was next to some dry leaves, and I was conscious of their musty smell, of the hard cold ground beneath me, of the gentle breeze that toyed with my hair. I heard a bird call somewhere in the distance, and the creaking of a tree branch.

But no shots rang out.

After a time, I began to feel foolish, sprawled ungracefully upon the ground. I got tentatively to my knees. When still nothing happened, I stood, brushing myself off.

Close on the heels of relief came anger. It seemed after all it really had been some careless hunter shooting at me. What was even worse, having heard my yell and realized his mistake, he hadn't even owned up to it like a man and come down to offer the apologies to which I felt entitled.

I suppose if I had been thinking more rationally, I would have scurried home along the path through the woods and looked upon it as another near calamity. But the aftershock of fear and indignation fed my anger, and without a thought that I might be walking into still greater danger, I started off for the hill from which I thought the shot had come.

Of course, there was no one there. At first glance it did not seem there was any evidence that anyone had been there. Then I saw something on the ground, shining in the pale sunlight just as my gold chain had done. I bent to pick it up and saw that it was what I first took to be a bullet and then realized was an empty shell.

So this was where he had stood. I turned and looked down at the pond. Yes, he had certainly had an easy target.

That thought held me to the spot for a moment. The gunman, whoever he had been, had indeed had a clear view of me as I had come around the pond. He could hardly have failed to see me or fired thinking I was anything but a human being. Neither the distance nor the surrounding land could create an illusion that I was a rabbit, or whatever hunters shot at here in the winter.

If that were so, then the incident had been no hunting accident, unless my man were particularly shortsighted.

But, if not an accident, then...then someone had deliberately tried to kill me.

The woods and hills about me suddenly seemed peopled with

threatening shadows. I glanced about uneasily, as if expecting to see someone lurking nearby, ready at any moment to pounce upon me.

There was no one. I was alone. But not far away, in a little patch of snow, was further evidence that I had not been alone for long. A man had walked this way, leaving his prints there in the snow.

A man, but not Mary Linton, not unless she were gallivanting about in vastly oversized boots. Hardly Jeff. No reason for it to be a servant.

Which left only David.

I walked in the direction indicated by the prints. There was another path here, running across the hills rather than through them as did the one I customarily took. But it led to the same place, back to Morgan house. I had not known of this higher path, but I could see that it was actually faster. One could leave the house after someone else, take this path while the other took the low, winding one through the woods, and easily be at the pond sooner.

I found no further prints, but there was little snow left along this path. I arrived back at the house without further incident.

Mrs. Evans looked relieved to see me back so soon. "I'm glad to see you made it this time without any more bad accidents," she said, giving a little laugh.

"Yes, so am I." There was no need to alarm her with my story of the shooting. I did not believe it had been caused by a foolish hunter, and that left only one other possibility.

I shed my coat and scarf, leaving them in the hall closet. In the game room I had already noticed a collection of weapons ranging from an assortment of guns to a Zulu knobkerrie and a seventeenth century halberd. On an impulse I went into that room.

I had paid little attention to the weapons before. Hunting was not a sport that evoked my admiration. Now I studied the walls with new interest.

Flanking the antlered head of a deer were two rifles and a

pair of knives in ornate sheathes. There are ways, I remembered from my reading, to tell if a gun had been fired recently, but I did not know what they were.

I touched one of the weapons. The rifle barrel was as cold as ice, although the room was comfortably warm. I touched the other. It felt warm to the touch, at room temperature.

The first one, then, had been out of doors quite recently. I pretty well thought I knew where.

I went back to the closet in the hall and looked at the garments hanging inside. I found what I was looking for almost at once.

David's coat had also been outside recently. The fabric was still cool to the touch.

CHAPTER TWENTY-SEVEN

Fresh snow began to fall and the temperature to drop. The first snowflakes came in timid wisps that melted a minute or two after they touched the ground but as the temperature continued to descend, they fell with more confidence, remaining on the ground, quickly creating a blanket of whiteness.

I sat by my window, watching the whiteness swirl down from above. The door to my room was locked. It would remain so until that time came to go down to prepare Jeff's dinner.

But even so, the air seemed charged with a current of danger. I could no longer deceive myself that I had been the target of a succession of accidents. The threat to my life was as real as the threat to Jeff's.

I had to fight the urge to panic, to flee the house at once. The simple truth was I would be in danger until I was on the train and on my way out of the town of Elsinore. If I waited and left tomorrow with Jeff, there would be at least the initial safety, however slim, of being two instead of one alone. They could not very well pick off two of us with stray bullets.

That we would leave the following day I was quite determined. If Jeff flatly refused to leave, then I would have to go without him. But I felt confident that, if I remained firm in my resolution, he would come with me. I would then have discharged my responsibility to him, and I would be done with this entire affair.

So I had only one more night to remain in the house, and nothing to concern myself with but seeing that no more accidents occurred. If I kept to the relative safety of my room as much as possible, and avoided going out of the house of all, I should have little cause for alarm. No matter how angry or desperate they might become, they could hardly slice me up with daggers in the presence of the servants.

On that cheery note, I applied myself to the task of repairing the chain on my pendant, so that I could put it on again.

Shortly before dinner time, I went in to see Jeff. He was in bed, sitting up, reading a book. He truly did look like he had recovered from his "illness", and that thought cheered me a little. I could see absolutely no reason for delays in our departure.

"Still determined to go tomorrow?" he asked when I came in, as if he had been reading my mind.

"Quite," I said. "There's a train that leaves just about noon. That should work out very nicely for us."

He chuckled softly, setting aside his book. "You were always as tough as nails once you had made up your mind to something."

"Then you know it's no use arguing about this."

"All right, all right," he said with a placating gesture. "I know when I'm beaten. I'll get out of bed tomorrow, even if I feel that I'm about to cross over. And I'll drive us into the train station in time for the noon train to New York City. Satisfied?"

"Yes," I said, smiling in the face of his teasing. I was relieved to know that he had accepted my decision. It eased some of the tension I had been feeling. For some reason I'd had a premonition that he might delay us, although it was silly to think that he should want to stay any longer than was necessary.

When I left him to go down to the kitchen, however, my sense of malaise returned. I was glad for the bright lights in the kitchen, for Mrs. Evans efficient comings and goings, and the bubbling good humor of the cook.

Both the latter and the young girl who came up from town to serve dinners expressed their regret at hearing I would soon be leaving, with no mention of my reason for doing so (which rather suggested that had an idea), and both wished me well.

"I was saying to Mrs. Evans just the other day," the cook said, hands folded under her bosom, "it's like a miracle the way you got the Mister healed. Why if I was to take sick myself, I'd want you right there looking after me."

"Thank you," I said, "but I'm afraid time did most of the healing. I only acted as an agent."

I was thinking with some inner amusement that it was as well for me that I had come to a particularly healthy household. It would have caused a great deal of difficulty if the servants had been plagued with illnesses that I could do nothing at all to cure.

* * * * * * *

The dinner for the evening was a hearty stew of beef and lamb with vegetables, made all the more appetizing by the snow now falling hard beyond the windows. On a genuinely blustery winter day, nothing seems quite so delicious as a hot stew with freshly baked bread, its aroma perfuming the kitchen.

I brought Jeff a mug of milk with his and a big slice of apple cobbler. His appetite, almost nonexistent when I had first come to the house, had returned with a vengeance in the past few days, which I took to be a good sign.

By the time I had carried the steaming, richly scented tray to his room and set out his meal, my own appetite was voracious. I returned to the kitchen and hungrily prepared my own tray to take up to my room.

"You're welcome to eat right here in the kitchen if you like," Mrs. Evans said, indicating the big round table at one end of the room.

"Thank you, but I like to listen to music while I eat." When I had taken to spending so much time in my room, Mrs. Evans had remembered that the attic contained an old rarely used phonograph and an assortment of long playing records.

I had, with proper permission of course, brought them down

to my room. Among the old fashioned platters were several of the classics that I loved, so that I had music when I desired it. I found that it helped to soothe any emotional turmoil that I was experiencing. It was easy to lose oneself in the drama of great music.

Back in my room I selected some records and put them on the turntable, adjusting the volume so that it would not disturb anyone else. My fire had been laid already, so I had only to light it to have that welcome glow.

I went into the bathroom connected to my room to wash my hands

When I came out again, Jeff was in my room, by my dinner tray. "Hello," he said, looking around. "I was hunting for some salt."

"There was some on your tray."

"Was there? I didn't notice it. Let me look." He went out, and a moment later opened the door a crack to say that he had found it after all.

Thank heaven I would soon be done with playing nursemaid, I thought, perhaps a little uncharitably. I sat down to what I hoped would be my last dinner and my last evening in the house.

Dinner over, I carried both the trays down to the kitchen, inquired once more after his health (I wanted no relapses there) and my chores were ended.

I had been reading once again Alice's Adventures Through the Looking Glass, in a lovely illustrated edition I had found in the library. I curled up in the big chair with Chopin playing on the phonograph and began to read.

Alice's adventures were as amusing and fresh each time I read them. The book had always been a particular favorite, but this time it gave me a queer sensation to read of the poor White King, lifted about by an invisible hand, much to his consternation.

I could not help but feel that I too, had been manipulated by some invisible, incomprehensible force, and I felt every bit as bewildered and frightened by it as he had.

"My dear," he told his queen afterward, "I turned cold to the very ends of my whiskers," to which she dutifully replied that he had no whiskers.

When I read of Alice's anxiety, I thought, like the Red Queen, "My dear, I've known anxiety compared with which that would be calming."

My eyelids began to droop.

...Alice never could quite make out, in thinking it over afterwards, how it was that they began. All she remembers is that they were running hand in hand, and the queen went so fast that it was all she could do to keep up with her. And still the queen kept crying, "Faster! Faster!" But Alice felt she could not go faster, though she had no breath left to say so.

I had no breath. I seem to be going faster and faster and getting nowhere, and I did not know how it all began.

"Faster," the Red Queen cried. "Don't try to talk."

"Don't try to talk."

I had no breath....

The room swam. I felt as if I had been spinning about and about in a giant vortex. My fingers worked as if to grab hold of something, anything, to steady myself. Everything in my line of vision was blurred and distorted, and I blinked and squinted, trying to see.

"Don't try to talk."

But it wasn't the Red Queen at all, it was Jeff, leaning close over me. And I wasn't through the looking glass door nor even in my chair, but flat on my bed.

Then it began again, the horrible, sweeping waves of pain and nausea, breaking over me like a pounding surf. I clutched at his hand and heard someone screaming and realized with horror that the screams were my own.

Consciousness tried to escape me. I reached out, grabbing it in my fingers, trying to hold it close, but it eluded me again and I ran after it.

Not the Red Queen this time but the White Knight, laughing. I ran toward him but the more I ran the farther away he was.

Only, I wasn't chasing him, he was chasing me, and when I tried to flee from him, I got closer and closer. He stabbed out with his lance, and the pain shot through me, like a flame from the underworld.

"Hold on, for god's sake hold on."

My room again, the ceiling spinning and tilting, and somewhere far away Jeff's face and voice. I knew that if I could reach him I would be all right but he drifted farther and farther away.

It came crashing through the fog of pain and nausea, the truth about what was happening. I had been through all this before, only it had been reversed. Then it had been Jeff who was sick, almost dying, and I had tried to pull him back from that dark abyss. This time it was I who was stricken. Even as I sank into unconsciousness again, I knew that I had been poisoned.

CHAPTER TWENTY-EIGHT

"Do you hear the snow against the window panes, kitty? How nice and soft it sounds! Just as if someone was kissing the window all over outside. I wonder if the snow loves the trees and fields, that it kisses them so gently? And then it covers them up snug, you know, with a white quilt...."

I opened my eyes. The light sent a bolt of pain crashing through my head, and it was a moment before I could open them again.

I saw the window first, and the snow falling beyond it, "kissing the window all over outside...." I winced when I tried to turn my head.

"Easy," Jeff said. He put a hand to my forehead. His hand felt cold and seemed to ease the pain somewhat

"Easy," he said again.

"Jeff...." My voice was hardly even a whisper. My lips and throat felt parched and raw.

"Don't try to talk," he whispered, leaning close. "You're going to be all right. The worst of it is past and I'm going to stay right here. Try to rest now, please."

I closed my eyes again and sank down into the darkness that had been hovering close at hand.

The pain was less when I woke again, and it was dark in the room. I tried to clear my mind enough to be able to think. Dark, light, dark.

I had taken sick Thursday night. It had been Friday when I returned to consciousness earlier. This must be Friday night. So

Morgan House had defeated me after all and my determination to leave on Friday. I was still here, perhaps for the rest of my life.

* * * * * * *

When I woke the third time, I knew I had recovered. But I felt as if I had been run through a washing machine. My limbs were nearly lifeless, they were so weak. I could only open my eyes and stare up at the ceiling. It was day again, presumably Saturday.

"Feeling better?" It was Jeff's voice again. I turned my head and there he was, sitting by the bed. He had moved the big old chair over from the fireplace, and it looked as if he had been camping out here. A quilt lay across one arm of the chair, and a pillow had dropped beside it on the floor.

He saw the glance. "Oh, don't worry," he said with a grin. "Mrs. Evans has supervised all the personal details. But I kept an eye out just the same."

And that, I thought ungratefully, ought to clinch it so far as what David thought about my relationship with Jeff.

That's being unkind, I scolded myself at once. Jeff had probably saved my life. Thank heaven he had known what the sickness was and how to handle it.

"Thank you," I whispered, through lips that still felt parched.

"Oh, she's awake," Mrs. Evans said from the doorway. She bustled into view. "Mercy, miss, you've given us a fright, you have. I thought we'd seen the last of you, I really did, but Mr. Linton here, he never gave up hoping and looking over you, and hasn't he performed just the same miracle you performed for him, bringing you right back to life?"

She said all of this in one breath, at the same time feeling my forehead for a fever, plumping up my pillow, and pouring some water from a pitcher by the bed into a glass.

"Drink this," she said, putting a hand behind my shoulders to help me to sit.

The water was cool and refreshing and soothed some of the dry taste in my throat.

"The very same as Mr. Linton," Mrs. Evans said, clucking her tongue. "I expect one of those virus things. Must have caught it from him."

Jeff and I exchanged rueful glances.

By afternoon I was able to sit up in bed, wrapped in my old cotton robe. Mrs. Evans brought me a mirror from the dresser, and I had my first look at the havoc the illness had wreaked on me. I looked as if I had aged ten years. My face was nearly as white as the sheets on the bed and lined with strain. My hair hung limp and straight, the yellow bleached nearly to whiteness. I did indeed look as if I had come close to death.

"Mr. David has asked after you constantly," Mrs. Evans said. I was alone with her. Jeff had at last to go to his own room for some proper sleep, now that he was certain I had pulled through. "He says that as soon as you feel up to it, he would like to see you."

"If he sees me like this it'll give him nightmares," I said, making a face at my own reflection in the glass.

"Pooh, I don't suppose he's expecting you to look like a movie star after what you've been through."

I bit my lip. "Bring me that case on the dresser. Yes, that's it, the makeup." I did not as a rule wear much makeup, but I felt that I needed it just now. Some lipstick and a little powder helped, without performing the miracles I would have wished for.

"Send Mr. David up," I said, running a brush through my hair.

He came in a few minutes after Mrs. Evans left. He looked shy and hesitant as he stood just inside the doorway. "Are you feeling all right?" he asked.

"I don't exactly feel like dancing in the streets, if that's what you had in mind," I replied. "But, yes, I do feel better."

He closed the bedroom door and came closer to the bed. He looked so very concerned that I could not imagine it was only feigned. Yet this was the surely the man who had fired upon me in the woods.

None of it seemed to make sense to me. It was like the pond, dark and frozen over, but beneath that smooth, crystalline surface was a world that was terrible and dangerous. The atmosphere in this house was the same. It had nearly cost me my life on several occasions now, and I was still not free of danger.

How could I equate that danger, though, with this anxious looking man standing above me now, so plainly concerned for my well-being?

"Chris," he said, speaking calmly but with an underlying intensity that made his words seemed passionate, "I know you don't care for me—no, don't interrupt me just yet, let me get this said—I know you love Jeff. I've been a fool and unforgivably rude as well, to try to push myself on you the way I have. I swear to you, I won't do that again."

He paused for a moment, as if searching for just the right words to express himself. "But I've come up to beg you to let me take you away from here."

My eyebrows went up but he hurried on. "Not as a lover. You don't have to be afraid of that, I won't make any advances. But, dammit—something's wrong here, in this house. I don't know what it is even but it's real and it's dangerous. There have been too many things happening, too many accidents.

"Maybe the house does have a curse on it. I don't know. But I'm afraid to let you stay here. I have to go into town, but I want to take you with me. Once you're there, you can do what you want. Meet Jeff, live your own life. I won't try to interfere. But I want to see that you get there safely. Will you come with me, please?"

He had taken my hand in his, squeezing it fiercely. It may have been that, it may have been the obvious sincerity of his concern, or the evidence that he really did love me. And part of it was certainly a result of the strain I had been under.

Whatever brought it on, I began quite unexpectedly to cry, deep in my throat at first and then with great sobs that wracked my body. I fell into the protective circle of his great arms laying my head against his chest, and gave myself up to the near hysteria that had overcome me.

"There, there," he said, stroking my hair tenderly. "It's going to be all right."

"Oh, David," I sobbed, no longer able to restrain myself. "I've been so afraid. I thought you.... And Mary...."

"Mary? What on earth has she got to do with anything?"

My sobs had begun to diminish. He held me away from him and looked into my tear-stained face. "What exactly have you been afraid of?"

I knew that I ought to keep my silence. I knew by every kind of logic that David must be a part of the danger that surrounded me. Another day, until I could manage to get out of bed, and I would be gone, and all of this would be ended. Surely, I could hold on that long.

But I couldn't and I knew that as well. I had tried to restrain my love for him, and I could not. Now I had to throw myself on his mercy, trust in the love I was certain he felt for me. Out of all the darkness and confusion, I was at least certain of our love. I had to believe in that, and in him.

I sniffled and said, as calmly as I was able, "Darling, Mary's trying to kill Jeff."

He was stunned by that statement, as well he might be. "Kill him? What on earth do you mean by that?"

"She's been trying to murder him." It was putting it boldly, brutally, but I was beyond subtlety just now. "With poison. Arsenic, in his food."

He let go of me and gave his head a shake. "This must be some sort of macabre joke," he said. He looked at me again and saw that I wasn't joking. "Chris, have you any idea what you're saying? Mary's wildly in love with her husband, for some crazy reason that I assure you I'll never understand. She would no more try to kill him than she would try to fly to the moon."

"But I assure you, it's true." I was quite sober now. I knew I must convince him of what I was saying.

His eyes narrowed. "Look, you've been through quite an ordeal. Being sick and all. Maybe we ought to discuss this later, when your mind is a little clearer."

I drew my shoulders back and brought my chin up. "My mind is quite clear enough David. This isn't something that just occurred to me during this illness of mine. And you might as well know the whole story while we're at it. This illness of mine was nothing more nor less than arsenic poisoning."

He jumped to his feet. "Chris, you can't possibly mean what you're saying!"

"I know the symptoms quite well. I've been nursing Jeff through a prolonged case of the same illness."

He was pacing up and down the room, looking increasingly bewildered. "And you think that Mary...no, it's too incredible. You can't know what you're saying."

"I had his tea analyzed before I came here, the tea Mary used to fix for him herself every day. It contained arsenic, a dosage sufficient to make him increasingly sick over a long period of time, eventually to kill him. You're going into New York. If you like, I'll give you the name of the pharmacist who had the tea analyzed for me. I'll write a note to him, giving him my permission to tell you about it. The tea was poisoned, David. It's no figment of my imagination, and no result of having been poisoned myself."

He stopped in the middle of the room. In the pause I could hear the clock over my fireplace ticking.

"And you think Mary poisoned you as well, night before last, that would be?" I nodded "How, in god's name?"

I started to speak and stopped, thinking back. I had so taken for granted that she was responsible that I had not until now given any thought to how it had been accomplished.

"I brought Jeff's dinner up on the tray," I said, thinking aloud. "Then I went back to the kitchen for my own dinner. I took it from the dishes that would be served to the family. I brought it upstairs. I went into my bathroom to freshen up...."

"Mary was in the dining room with me," he said.

"And when I came back in this room, Jeff was here. He'd come over to see if I had any salt."

"That vulture," he said vehemently. "If there's any crime being done around here, I'll guarantee you one thing, he's the one doing it."

"Jeff?" I must have looked completely incredulous.

"Why not Jeff? Are you so blinded to the facts that you can accuse Mary of coldly trying to kill the two of you, but you think he'd be incapable of it? That man would strangle his own mother if it suited his purpose."

"That may well be true," I said, and in my own mind I rather thought it was, "but it would make no sense at all to think that Jeff is behind everything else that's happened."

"Everything? Is there more than the poisoning business?"

"That trap set in the woods. It might have been an accident, but I don't think so, and I don't believe it was Peter's carelessness, either. And just before I got sick, someone shot at me in the woods."

"Shot at you?"

"With a rifle. It might have been a careless hunter, but that's rather stretching coincidence, don't you think?"

"Why didn't you tell me about it at the time? Or about the poison?"

"I...it's all been so tenuous."

He ran a hand through his dark hair. "Whew. This is rather a lot to take in. You haven't stretched any of it a little, to...no, of course not, that's not your way." He was thoughtful for a moment.

"Then it has to be Jeff," he said. "I don't know what it's all about, but I know him for what he is, a heartless, scheming devil who married my sister for her money. There's nothing I'd put past him. If somebody's trying to murder you, take my word for it, it's him."

I leaned wearily back against the pillows. "Darling, make sense," I said. "Jeff would hardly be trying to kill himself with arsenic poisoning, would he? And if he were, he would not be likely to summon me up here to help him recover from it. And even granting all of that, what conceivable motive could he have for wanting to kill me? And if by some stretch of the imagination he can be given a motive, it makes no sense at all for him to poison me on one hand and then spend two days helping me to recover from the poison on the other hand. No, darling, you can't have it both ways, don't you see?"

He slammed his fist into the palm of his hand, looking increasingly angry. "No, I don't see, but I know my sister and I know Jeff. Mary might be cruel in many ways, but she is not the murderous type, take my word for it."

"And I suppose next you'll be saying it was Mrs. Evans," I said, more curtly than I intended. My head had begun to ache again. He was right of course, none of this made any sense, it hadn't from the beginning.

But he was let letting his dislike for Jeff, a dislike which obviously bordered on hatred, affect his judgment. I did not much care for Jeff's character either, but it was as plain as could be that he hadn't been trying to do me in, unless one assumed he was merely a homicidal maniac, and that was stretching my imagination completely beyond the limits.

David came back to the bed again, seizing my hand in an impulsive gesture. "Come away with me, now," he said, speaking urgently. "I'll carry you down to the car. Once you're safely away from here and away from any danger, then we can look into this matter fully."

I shook my head. Every fiber of my being was urging me to do as he said, to throw myself into his arms, give all of the responsibility over to him. I need concern myself no more with fear and danger and trying to unravel the knot of mystery here.

"I can't," I cried, wishing I could make him understand. "I have a promise, to Jeff."

He let go of my hand and jumped to his feet again. "Jeff, Jeff, is that all you can think of?"

The outburst was so violent that I could think of nothing to say.

"You are in love with him, aren't you?" he demanded.

"No, I—"

"Then come with me, now."

I sighed and closed my eyes. "I can't. Don't you see, I'd never forgive myself if anything happened after I had run out on him?"

"You can't have it both ways either, Chris." He was speaking in anger, and I knew it, but the words stung anyway. "You can't have Jeff and me. You'll have to decide. Which do you want?"

"I want you," I said, in anguish. "But I can't leave him here, David, I just can't, you must understand."

"I do," he said in a voice suddenly turned cold. "I do understand indeed." He turned and went to the door. He paused as he opened it. For a moment I thought he would see it differently and come back to me.

But he did not. He went out without another word, slamming the door.

I wanted to call to him and very nearly did. I even threw back the covers on an impulse, as if I would run after him and beg him to understand.

But I neither called nor went after him. It would be no use. He was in a temper, and nothing I would say just now would convince him. And what could I say anyway? None of it made any more sense to me than it did to him. He was right in everything he had said about Jeff. I couldn't quarrel with his views on Jeff's character. And certainly he knew Mary better than I did.

And he was quite right in finding my story incredible. I had been living through it and yet it seemed to me like some nightmare fantasy, and not a real experience.

I fell across the cool surface of the sheets and began to cry.

CHAPTER TWENTY-NINE

I was still crying when Jeff, having awakened from his sleep, came in to see me.

"What's the matter?" he asked, seating himself on the edge of the bed and putting a consoling hand on my shoulder.

"Oh, Jeff, I want to leave," I said, sobbing. "I want to leave now, this moment."

"So do I, but let's face it, you're doing well to sit up. You just aren't up to making the trip into New York City."

"I am," I cried. I tried to sit up and get out of the bed, but of course my strength was not yet adequate to that task, and I fell back weakly.

"Now, there," he said, patting my arm. "You're not to work yourself into a lather. By tomorrow I'm confident you'll be able to get out of the bed. I promise you, as soon as you can manage to stand and move around, we'll leave. If need be, we'll take one of the cars and drive all the way into New York. Trust me, will you?"

I sniffled and nodded. I could do nothing else but trust him, after all.

But I was determined that I would linger no longer than was absolutely necessary, and with this in mind, I set myself to the task of regaining sufficient strength to get out of bed. When Jeff had gone, I made myself sit up, and not like a limp rag, either, but straight and firm, with shoulders back. I would not allow myself the luxury of playing convalescent.

In the afternoon I was able, with some help from Mrs. Evans, to get out of bed and go sit in the chair by the fireplace.

"Well, well," Jeff said when he found me there. "Looks like we're making a fast recovery."

"It can't be fast enough to please me."

"What she needs is some rest and lots of good food," Mrs. Evans said.

I smiled at Jeff. She could not know how important the question of food was. Each time I ate, even knowing that Jeff was keeping his eye out for me, I felt a twinge of uneasiness. If I could have done without eating for a day, I would have done so. But I needed the strength that food would provide.

The snow had begun to fall again. I lay in bed in the dark that night and watched it fall. It gave a sense of peace and calm, blurring the jagged edges of the world and softening the lines. And the very silence of its falling, unlike the pattering of rain, gave it a soothing air.

In the morning it had turned the world white. I looked out upon an estate carved of crystal and fluff.

I was able to get out of bed in the morning without assistance. When Mrs. Evans came to see if I was ready for breakfast, I was already dressed and seated in my chair awaiting her.

"Heavens, miss, she exclaimed. "You look almost as good as new."

I laughed because I had examined myself closely in the mirror and I knew only too well that I looked no such thing. But I did feel like a million dollars in comparison to the day before. And although I was still weak, and my legs tended to feel rubbery when I tried to walk, I was confident that Jeff and I could manage the trip into the city.

"Is Mr. David still in the house?" I asked while I poured myself some coffee, hot and black.

"Oh no, miss," she said, giving no indication that she attached any significance to the question. "He left early yesterday, shortly after he was up to see you. Said he didn't know just when he would be back."

"I see." I sipped the coffee and hid my feelings behind the

cup's rim. "And Mr. Linton?"

She looked truly pleased to be able to tell me, "He's having breakfast downstairs this morning, miss, for the first time in I don't remember how long. And it's you we have to thank for that, if you'll pardon my saying so. Shall I send for him?"

I thought for a moment. "No," I said, "I think I shall join him."

"Oh, Miss, do you think you ought?"

"I don't know if I ought, but I know that I would like. I'll tell you what, you can help me down the stairs, and if I find it's too much of an ordeal, we can turn around and come back."

She looked unconvinced, but it was not her nature to argue and she could see how determined I was to make this trip. It wasn't only a matter of pride, either. I wanted Jeff to see for himself that I was truly able to leave today.

"I expect you'll be leaving before too long," Mrs. Evans said as we started down the hall. She kept a steadying hand on my arm, but I was able to manage fairly well.

"I hope so," I said, not wanting to spend on conversation the breath that I might need for walking

"Looks like you're going to see some real upstate weather before you go."

"Yes, that was quite a snow last night." We had reached the stairs. Here I had not only Mrs. Evans but the banister to support me. It was just as well, too. My strength had begun to fade.

"It isn't over," she said, talking on as if she wanted to distract me from the effort I was expending. "The storm, I mean. I was just out back. It's started falling again, and the wind is blowing up a good one."

Our progress along the downstairs hall was slower than it had been upstairs, but at last we reached the dining room.

Near the door, I paused. "Thank you for your help," I said in a low voice. "But I want to walk into the room under my own steam, if I may."

"I understand." She let go of me and stepped aside.

I stood for a moment more, taking in a deep breath,

summoning up all my strength. It was the sort of dramatic entrance any actress would have envied. The last thing I wanted to do was spoil it. I would not even allow myself to think of the possibility of falling flat on my face. I had a fleeting, quickly disposed of vision of myself lying across the breakfast table, face buried in Jeff's morning grapefruit.

He stood up as I came into the room. "Chris," he exclaimed, astonished. "Lord, I didn't even know you were up."

"I...I wanted to surprise you," I said, a bit breathlessly.

That was as much as I managed. My legs gave out then. He leaped forward to catch me, so I did not land in the grapefruit but in Jeff's arms.

"Aren't you happy to see me walking," I asked, leaning heavily against him.

"Delighted."

Something clicked, I don't quite know what. In the past, when I had been infatuated with him, every word he spoke had been taken at face value. It simply never occurred to me he would lie to me in any way.

But I knew him better now. I had no illusions about his character or his honesty. He had none, or very little. The truth to him was whatever worked best to his advantage.

Moreover, he told his half-truths and falsehoods with a polish that indicated the theater ought to have been more successful for him than it had. He told them so very well, in fact, that I could not help but know when he was telling them. He spoke then with the sort of brightness that was not usually there in his ordinary conversation, when he cared less what he said, or how it came out sounding.

So I could not help but be puzzled at this particular moment. Why should he lie about being delighted to see me walking? Why, indeed, should he be anything but delighted?

That he was not telling the truth I was quite certain, however. He was, I was quite sure of it, very much un-delighted.

I hadn't the time to really consider this puzzle, however, because I had no more than landed in his arms when I felt him stiffen and grow tense.

"My, what a cozy scene," Mary said from the doorway behind me.

CHAPTER THIRTY

I had always seen Mary Linton more or less under control. She had always been, regardless of her mood, inherently elegant and self-possessed, her hair beautifully coiffed, her face made up with a skill I could not but envy.

So, I was shocked to see her now. She wore little makeup, but that little had been so badly applied it gave her the grotesque appearance of a harridan from some poorly directed stage piece.

Vivid rouge had been rubbed over her white cheeks and a flash of lipstick smeared carelessly across for mouth. Her hair had hardly been combed, only pushed back from her face, so that untidy wisps stuck out here and there.

There was no mystery as to how she had managed to do so badly with her makeup. Although it was only a little after nine, I did not need the sight of the glass in her hand to tell me she had been drinking already, and more than just the one she held.

"You've been drinking," Jeff said in a tone of disgust.

She laughed, a dried, mirthless sound. "How brilliant of you to discern it. I suppose it shocks you." Her bleary eyes came to rest on me. "And you, Miss Goody-Two-Shoes, does it offend your delicate sensibilities?"

I knew it was pointless to take offense. "Perhaps you ought to ring for Mrs. Evans," I said to Jeff, "and have some coffee brought."

She laughed again. "How amusing. You think stealing another woman's husband is quite all right, no scruples when it comes to that. But a little drink to try to dull one's misery...."

"Mary, please...," Jeff started to say.

"Misery!" She screamed the single word of the top of her lungs. It seemed to reverberate through the room and the silence that followed.

She began to cry, softly at first and then with great choking sobs that shook her body.

"I think I ought to go to my room," I said to Jeff. "No, stay here, please. Just ring for Mrs. Evans, if you will, and I'll have her help me."

There was no need of course to ring for Mrs. Evans. I had forgotten she had been waiting outside to be sure I was all right and did not need her further support. She stepped into the doorway behind Mary, looking quite embarrassed by the entire scene.

But Mary was not yet finished with disencumbering herself of her feelings. "You," she said through her tears, pointing an accusing finger at me, "how can you be so cruel? Oh, I understand Jeff. I know he has no feelings for me, he never has. He's incapable of feeling love for anyone. But I love him, don't you understand that? I love him! I beg you, please don't take him away for me. I'll give you anything else, all the money you could want. This house if you want it, but not my husband, please." She began to sob again, her shoulders heaving.

"Go to her," I said to Jeff. He went, putting his arms about her and trying to comfort her. I did not linger to hear what they might have to say to one another in private. I only hoped he would be kind and patient.

* * * * * * *

Alone once more in my room, I sat for some time trying to regain my strength. Mrs. Evans brought some hot tea before leaving me to my own devices.

"It may be leftovers for lunch," she said as she started from the room. "Cook's worried about the storm and is talking about going home before it comes up any worse."

Beyond the window the storm had taken quite a turn for the worse. The snow that had been falling gently before was now lashing against the window in violently driven gusts. It was as dark as if it were twilight instead of mid-morning.

I had other problems on my mind, however, than whether lunch was freshly prepared or consisted of leftovers. I curled up in my chair, sipping the hot tea.

Sometime later I heard Jeff helping his wife along the hall past my room. They were talking in low voices. Even had I been inclined to eavesdrop, which I was not, I would not have been able to distinguish their words. He seemed to be consoling her, and I was grateful for that.

When they had gone by, I stirred myself to action once again. I had recovered sufficiently from my trip up and down the stairs that I could stand again and move about. My suitcases were in the closet in my room. I got them out, opening them up on the bed, and began slowly and carefully to pack my things.

I was nearly finished by the time, quite a bit later, that Jeff came into my room. "Packing already?" he asked, looking somewhat surprised.

"Yes. As you can see, I am able to get around, if a little cautiously. And I think that scene downstairs is evidence enough that we should go as soon as possible. There's the noon train, and if it's too late for us to catch that one, there's another about three. We can surely catch that."

"I'm not sure I ought to leave Mary in her present state."

I gave him a stern look. "Then I assume you'll have no objection to my leaving alone." My tone of voice could leave very little doubt as to whether that threat was idle or no.

"That's the way it lies, is it?" He smiled faintly, but again I had the impression of something false.

"I'm afraid so," I said stubbornly.

He shrugged and seemed to give in. "Perhaps you're right," was all he said. He left and I went back to my packing

I was long since finished and was beginning to think after all I would be going without him when he came into my room again

"Have you packed your things?" I asked him, of no mind to beat around the bush.

"It doesn't worry you, leaving Mary in the state she was in?"

"Mrs. Evans will see she is well taken care of," I said coldly.

"Mrs. Evans isn't here."

Something dark and fearful skirted the far reaches of my mind. "What do you mean, she isn't here? She was here no more than an hour or so ago."

"I sent her home. Rather, I gave her permission to leave, since she was afraid of not being able to get home later."

I remember the swirling clouds of snow beyond my window. I'd already begun to suspect what he was going to tell me.

"All of the servants are gone, actually. There's no one here but you and I and Mary."

I took a deep breath and said, "If you choose to stay with your wife that is your affair. But I for one have had all I want of this house and the funny goings-on here. I mean to leave today, now. Will you take me into town?"

He shook his head and said as one would speak to an impatient child, "Darling, must you be so difficult? I'm trying to explain to you, in as gentle a way as possible, that we can't leave. The storm has gotten too bad, a real blizzard. We'll have to wait it out."

I looked outside again. I could see nothing but what appeared to be a sheet of white, moving with each gust of wind. The world beyond had been obliterated from view.

I fought back a sudden feeling of panic. "Perhaps you must remain here," I said, hating myself because my voice sounded fearful even to my own ears, "but storm or no storm I mean to go. If you won't take me, I shall phone for a taxi."

His smile did seem more genuinely amused to this time. "You simply won't be convinced, will you? I'm afraid you won't phone for a taxi or anything else. The phone isn't working. Probably a line is down somewhere. No, my dear, we're here until the storm is over and probably for a while after that. And there's not a thing we can do about it."

CHAPTER THIRTY-ONE

I think I knew them. Something inside me said, but.... Aloud, I said, "yes, of course, I do see."

He breathed a little sigh of relief to see me backing down from my battle stance. "That's better," he said. "I was beginning to think you were ready to try hiking it, and I assure you, that gale out there would down a native. I told you, Mrs. Evans begged off early, and she's not exactly a scaredy-cat."

"I hope she did make it home all right," I said. "That does leave us on our own, then? Just you and I?"

"And Mary, but I'm afraid she's going to be asleep for quite a while. Why?"

"I was just thinking about lunch. Shall I plan on fixing it?"

He was tenderness and thoughtfulness all through. "Look, that's hardly right, is it? I mean, you've been through a devil of an ordeal. Why don't you just relax and make yourself comfortable. Leave everything else to me."

I gave in to his gentle persuasion. "All right," I said, letting myself relax. "You're the boss, it seems. And frankly, now that I know it's impossible for us to go, I don't mind admitting, it was a real strain to be up and about. I could do with a little rest after all, maybe even a nap before lunch."

"Now that's the girl," he said, brimming over with cheer. "You get yourself rested. When this storm's over, and we can leave safely, you'll want to have all your strength back."

"Jeff, we can leave just as soon as the roads are clear, can't we? I mean, you won't get all sentimental over Mary and decide to stay a while?"

He laughed that suggestion away. "Are you joking? I want to get away even more desperately than you do. I'm the one they've been after, remember?"

I laughed, too, because it was a silly idea. I was still smiling as he went out.

My smile vanished with the closing of the door. There wasn't any doubt of it, not the slightest. I had thought for a moment there that maybe I was mistaken this once, maybe I was reading his voice or his expression all wrong.

But I had never been more certain of anything in my life. Jeff had no intention of leaving Morgan House. He never had intended to. Nor did he intend for me to leave without him.

It was like a blow. David had been right, and I had been wrong. In some incredible way that I could not yet understand, all of this was Jeff's doing. He was responsible for all the things that had been happening. It was such an obvious truth, but I had refused to see it before. Yet it couldn't have been plainer.

My head was spinning. Thoughts, one contradicting the next, crashed through my mind. I took a deep breath.

"Easy, girl," I told myself. "You're verging on a good case of the heebie-jeebies."

I went to the phonograph and with deliberate slowness chose some records to play, and clicked on the machine. The turntable began to circle, the arm lifted, a record dropped and a second later music took over the room.

I sat down in my chair, listening to the flurry of piano notes— Chopin, the *Grande Valse Brillante*, all gaiety and brilliance with its affecting turns into minor in the middle section. The pianist was Brailowsky. His nimble fingers seem to bring the instrument to life. The notes sang, as they do for only the great interpreters.

I had to be mistaken. Obvious or not, Jeff's guilt defied all reason.

Guilty of what? Trying to kill himself? Utterly preposterous. Somebody else he might very well kill, but not the one person in the world of whom he was genuinely fond, himself.

He might very well kill somebody else—the phrase lingered. Me? Equally ridiculous. I'd already gone over that with David. There was simply no motive. Jeff was, after all, the one who had brought me up here and through trickery kept me here.

Yes, trickery, that he was guilty of, certainly. He had been keeping me here through one means or another. Of course, he couldn't have arranged for the storm, but it had fallen in well with his wishes.

But it was my poisoning that had really delayed our departure, and it was Mary who had poisoned me, wasn't it?

Brailowsky went into the bravura of the coda.

No, not Mary of all. David had told me that, and I had not accepted it. Of course it was true. She had been with him. Jeff had been here, with my food.

Could he have poisoned me? Yes, he was capable of doing whatever he took it in his head to do.

But surely not to murder me. There was no reason for that. Anyway, he had been the one to nurse me back to health. So he had poisoned me (accept that, try to work it out from there) not to kill me, but to keep me from leaving.

I was back where I had started, at the same blank wall. Jeff was the one who wanted to leave. He was the one, as he had said himself a short while before, who was in danger, the one they had been trying to kill.

But he had been lying, I was sure of it. He didn't want to leave.

And we were back at the beginning again. Why would he not want to leave, if they were trying to kill him? Because he had gone sentimental over Mary? It was possible but awfully thin.

"All right," I said to myself, "stop thinking so poorly of him and try that one on." He didn't want to leave Mary, regardless of what she had done. Maybe in some strange way all his own, he really loved her.

"And you won't admit that possibility," I told myself cruelly, "because he wounded your vanity by not loving you. Ergo, he couldn't possibly love anybody."

I talked myself into accepting the fact that he loved Mary. It followed that it might be hard for him to make himself leave her. At the same time, he was afraid because she had been trying to kill him. He wanted to keep me here for safety's sake, that theory went.

And so, I told myself sarcastically, he poisoned me and left me out of my head for two days to keep me here for protection. Pretty silly, that line of reasoning.

Chopin had ended. It was Tchaikovsky's turn now. For all its mistreatment at the hands of Tin-Pan Alley, the opening of the B flat concerto still gave me a thrill. The very germ of the introductory theme, heard as a peremptory figure for the horn. Thrice it commanded the listener's attention. Each time that emphatic chord hammered out by the full orchestra, punctuated its close. And then the whole melody suddenly unfolding in all its grandeur, carried by the orchestra amid that majestic chordal figuration of the piano.

The music swept through me, heightening the tension I was experiencing rather than diminishing it.

Start with what I knew, bare facts. They were trying to poison him, that much was certain. I'd had the tea analyzed myself, so I knew about that.

They who?

Rubenstein had taken the solo lead with the full blooded D flat major tune; there was the quasi cadenza episode, and the same tune was back, reiterated with even more of an over-whelming effect by the orchestra, while the pianist performed the crashing octave figuration.

David? No, my heart told me clearly and confidently there was no possibility of that. He might be stubborn, tempera-mental, even a fool in some thoroughly lovable ways. But he was no murderer. A sock in the eye was more his style anyway.

Mary, of course

The little nervous melodic passage began. Its fitful pattern— taken, so the story goes, from a song sung by blind beggars in a little village—brought me from my chair to pace the floor, rubbing my hands together as if they were cold.

The pair of lyrics themes came in, one plaintiff, the other, in the muted strings, tranquil and nostalgic.

I had been a fool, that was obvious. But I had come with a built in dislike and resentment for Mary. That and a five year old affection for Jeff had put me automatically on his side, looking at everything from the side of the fence on which he had skillfully placed me.

Mary was no murderess. David had told me that, but any fool should have been able to see it for herself. She had practically gone livid upon learning of Peter's trapping of animals on her property. The very thought of helpless animals caught, bleeding, dying had sickened her.

Murder her husband to keep him from leaving her? I had seen her this very morning, crazed with grief and drunk, and she had sobbed of her love for him and begged me not to take him from her.

I put my hands to my head and squeezed as if I could force the confusion within into some sort of comprehensible form.

Mary hadn't been trying to murder Jeff. David hadn't been doing it. I hadn't, and certainly Mrs. Evans and the servants hadn't. But that left no one but Jeff.

And the trap in the woods? Assuming it hadn't been an accident, who had set it where it might harm me? Who had a motive? Mary? Her shock had been too real when she learned about the traps afterward. I could not credit her with being that great an actress.

David? Eliminated from the list, same reasons as before.

Jeff? He was out of bed by them, able to get around. He could've gone in and out. He had told me himself that everyone else was out. No one would have seen him.

Who had fired at me in the woods? Not Mary. The footprint I had found had been of a man's boot.

David? Eliminate him for the same reason? He had been out, his coat was cold. But had he been in the same direction as I had been? Being out of doors did not prove that he had been shooting at me.

Jeff?

The music was well into the second movement now, with its serene opening melody for the flute, taken up afterward by the piano. Then came the pert and lilting little tune done by the violas and the cellos, taken, if one accepts the legend, from a little French chansonette, *il faut s'amuser, danser et rire*. Dance and laugh indeed.

I was going back and forth across the room, moving faster and faster as the music moved along, surging into the last movement, the finale. Building, soaring upward, the drama mounting and mounting with feverish yet dynamically controlled intensity. The orchestra and the pianist fought with one another, first one and then other to the fore.

If I had some proof, any sort of proof, something to give confirmation or prove a lie to the thoughts crashing through my mind. But what, and where to look?

Rubinstein began the dramatic octave run from low to the high piano register climaxed by the three powerful chords for the piano and the full orchestra.

The room burst into silence.

I knew suddenly where to look.

CHAPTER THIRTY-TWO

He was not in his room. I closed the door, trying to still the pounding of my heart. It was nearly dark in here. The draperies were closed, although my own room, with the draperies open to the storm outside, had not been much brighter.

I found the strongbox just where it had been before, under the bed. Exactly where, the thought came unbidden into my mind, he could get it, even when he was sick, without getting out of bed.

I had forgotten, until I took it from under the bed and set it down on top of the bedspread, that it was locked. Nor had I the slightest doubt that he kept the key with him at all times

I looked around quickly but there was nothing close at hand that looked a suitable for forcing a lock. I rattled it. It was not awfully strong looking, but certainly it was not going to yield to my frail hand.

I went back to my own room, automatically walking on tiptoe, but nothing there seemed to lend itself to the task either. I chewed ferociously on my lip. I would have to go downstairs to look for something.

Jeff was in the kitchen. I remembered that in the past he had enjoyed occasionally puttering around in the kitchen but it was a shock to see him now, a dishtowel for an apron, stirring a large pot on the stove.

"Umm, smells good," I said, sniffing the air as I came him. I had never realized that I had any acting talents, but he seemed to find nothing unusual in my manner or appearance.

"Slumgullion," he said, glancing over his shoulder. "The most I can promise is that it'll be hot. Looking for anything in particular?"

I started. I had been peering around trying to think where on earth the tools would be. I had forgotten Mrs. Evans had a little mirror hanging by the sink, presumably so she could keep an eye on things in the kitchen while she worked. Jeff had seen me in it.

"A screwdriver," I said, "and maybe a pair of pliers, if you know where to find them."

"Good lord, are you taking something apart?"

"Just my suitcase," I said, opening a drawer. It held an ominous selection of knives and gadgets but neither screwdriver nor pliers. "I'm having some trouble with the clasp."

"Let it go." He gave his attention back to the stew. "I'll fix it later. Here, taste this."

"I'll be simmering all afternoon, just like that stew, if I don't get at it." I came over to the stove, tasted, and opened another drawer. "Umm, good. Where do you suppose she keeps things like that anyway?"

"All right, blast it." He chuckled. "If you will be the liberated female. I think she has a few things in that cupboard over there." He pointed with a spoon.

I found both pliers and screwdriver and started from the kitchen.

"What's it need to fix it?"

I stopped short. "Oh, just some hammering and twisting, I think."

"No, I meant the stew." He laughed. "Does it need more salt, do you think?"

I couldn't very well tell him it had tasted like pure arsenic to me. "Just a dash, maybe," I said, and made a hasty escape.

The lock gave with one hard twist of the screwdriver. I lifted the lid and, taking up the box, opened the contents upon the bed.

It was there, of course, just as I had already guessed it must be. It was in a small canister, astonishingly small for the damage

I knew it could do, and appropriately marked with the word "poison," and the symbol of the skull and crossbones. It was labeled AS203.

That hasty library reading I had done came back to me in a flash. This whitish powder was arsenic. The sort of arsenic used in a glassworks. Like the Morgan glassworks that Jeff had taken such an interest in, for a time.

And still it made no sense. All right, he had the poison, not Mary. But why? Why nearly kill himself, nearly kill me, and see that both of us recovered? There had to be some logical explanation, but it still eluded me.

I heard his footsteps almost too late. There was no time to get out of his room and back to my own, scarcely time enough to think of hiding. His room had its own bath. The door stood open just a few feet away. I literally flew into it, flattening myself against the wall behind the half-open door.

It wasn't reasoning that drove me to hide from him rather than being found now in his room. It was blind instinct. The same instinct that had told me earlier in my room that, whatever reason said, Jeff was my enemy, the source of danger, and not Mary. I heard him come into his bedroom and pause.

You blooming idiot, I said silently to myself. I had trapped myself in the bathroom. If he came in here I had no way of escape and no way to hide myself. And it was going to look all the more peculiar for him to discover me trying to hide than had he merely found me in his room.

My heart was pounding, threatening to break free from my chest. I strained my ears but could hear nothing. Would the floor creak if he came across the room? I tried to remember but my thoughts were too scattered.

I let out my breath in one loud rush. He had gone back out. I stepped out of the bathroom, listening. Yes, this time I had guessed it right. He had gone across the hall to my room. He opened the door and called my name.

"Chris? You in here?"

I took a deep breath, stepped into the middle of his bedroom, and called back, very loudly, "Jeff? Are you looking for me? I'm over here, in your room."

I heard him start back across the hall—I knew that floor creaked—and in that awful instant before he opened his door again, when there was no time of all in which to do anything about it, I saw what he must have seen himself a minute ago.

There, atop his bed was his strongbox, its lock broken, its contents, poison and all, scattered about it.

CHAPTER THIRTY-THREE

I started toward the dresser. He came in, his gaze following me away from the bed. "I was in here just a minute ago," he said. "Where were you, under the bed?"

I hoped that my look of innocence came off. "In the bathroom. I heard you come in, but when I came out to say hello, you had gone right back out."

He looked as if he had bought it. There was nothing menacing or threatening in his look or his tone. Maybe, I thought he didn't see. If I can keep him looking at me, until we leave the room....

"Lose something?" I was rummaging around the top of his dresser. "A handkerchief. I thought maybe I'd left it in here. Nope, not a sign of it here, either."

"As long as you're in here, there's something I want to show you." He came across the room past me to the closets and lifted two big suitcases out.

"All packed," he said, grinning at me. "I wanted you to see for yourself, I wasn't just putting you on. As soon as the weather clears up, were on our way."

"It won't be long," I said. All sorts of awful little creatures were clawing and throwing themselves at the cage of my mind, trying to break in. I dared not let them in where I could see them. I had to continue smiling, looking unconcerned and confident.

"You may as well see the rest of it, too," he said. He came to the dresser and, opening one of the top drawers, took out some papers, handing them to me with a look of genuine amusement.

It was a moment or so before I could grasp the significance. I held train tickets to New York from Elsinore. That much would have seemed reasonable. But the airline tickets from New York to London were quite a shock.

"And my passport," I said, holding it up. "How on earth did you get this?"

"If you're willing to pay enough, you can hire people to do almost anything."

It clicked in my mind. "You broke into my apartment!"

"Not in person. Sort of by mail, and by telephone in a manner of speaking."

I must have continued to look genuinely shocked, because he added, "It was a little presumptuous of me, wasn't it? I hope you're not too sore."

"I...but why on earth?"

"Can't you guess?"

"You...you want me to go to London with you." It was not a question, since after all that much was obvious. We had never discussed any such possibility, though. I had never intended anything more than seeing Jeff safely to New York, where we would part company.

He was still smiling, waiting for me to take the rest of this in. I did, all of it. It was suddenly as clear in my mind as if a flash of lightning had illuminated the landscape. I saw it all in macabre detail.

Thank heaven I was looking down at documents in my hand. My expression must have been ghastly.

Of course, Jeff had never meant to leave Mary. Jeff, give up all this money and luxury? Preposterous. I could well see his wanting give up Mary, though, and contemplating her murder to get her out of the picture.

But in the end, it hadn't been her murder that had been needed. He had practically explained it all to me himself in the reverse fashion. Knowing him, it had probably amused him greatly to come so close to giving me the key to the mystery. Mary, he had told me himself, did not dare to try to kill him once it was known that he and I were lovers, because she would be the first and most obvious suspect.

That worked in many ways. He couldn't have risked killing his wealthy wife, either, without making himself the prime suspect.

But if he had a mistress, with whom he was conducting an illicit affair—worse, with whom he was planning to run away— and the mistress were killed, it would be the jealous wife, not Jeff, who would be accused. No one would ever suspect him of killing his mistress. And there was so much evidence against Mary, enough to see her hanged.

It was no more than a second in which I saw all of these things, fitted together into a diabolical scheme to which I was the keystone. Mary's drunkenness, that had worked out well for him. Scenes between Mary and me, to which the servants would testify. The suitcases, all packed. The tickets, the passports. Mary driven to desperation. Jeff being poisoned as the evidence could later show. The attempt to poison me, thwarted by Jeff. The love letters....

He was going to kill me. He was going to kill me and make it seem Mary had done it. And that was why he had not wanted me to leave before everything was ready.

Now, the stage was set.

Somehow, I got a smile on my face. I didn't have to work to make it seem a little tentative, nor did I have to pretend to be a little nervous.

I looked up at him under veiled lashes. "Jeff, I...I'm not sure if I'm getting this exactly right, what these tickets and these passports mean. I hope they mean what I think."

"You hope?"

I had two things in my favor. One, he didn't know yet that I was on to him. And secondly, most important of all, there was that incredible vanity of his. If I could carry this off, it was going to give him a great deal of gratification. Enough, I hoped, to keep his mind off of what he was planning, until....

"This is kind of a difficult thing to put into words. Especially for a woman. I mean, usually the man takes the initiative in this sort of thing. Oh, damn. You do see what I'm driving at, don't you?" My eyelashes fluttered. How on earth did they play these scenes in the movies? At the moment, I could only remember the murder sequences, not the seductions.

"I think so," he said. He was already beginning to look damnably pleased with himself, for which I genuinely loathed him.

"You know I've never stopped loving you," I said, all in one quick rush of words, before I could choke on them.

"You've been pretty cool since you came here."

"I know. Well, look, I had a right to be miffed, didn't I? A girl doesn't like being jilted and neglected for five years. When I came here and saw you again, I.... Honestly, I thought I hated you. But afterward I realized I couldn't have, could I, because I wouldn't have come back to try to help you if I had." And how did you know, bless you, that I'd fall for that line you handed me? Had I always been a pushover?

"And you realized after you came that you're in love with me?"

"It doesn't sound very romantic put like that," I said with a little moue. "But, being around you again day, in and day out, thrown together, as it were. Oh, Jeff did you really mean for us to run off to London together? Because if this is some sort of proposal, the answer is yes."

I don't know which was worse, trying to carry off this nonsensical scene of the heartsick girl in love all over again with the irresistible man, or what must inevitably come next. That it was inevitable I had realized all along. Still, it gave me a start when he came grinning across the room to me, grabbing me in his arms.

"Darling," I said, putting a hand against his chest. "Don't you think we ought to wait until...?"

"We're alone in the house."

"Mary...."

"Isn't going to bother us for a long time." He found my mouth. How much encouragement did you have to give her, I wondered, to be sure she'd stay passed out for the day?

His eyes were a little puzzled. "Not exactly passionate," he said, breathing huskily.

"It's...such a change in things," I said, biting my lip. "I haven't quite gotten used to...necking with a married man."

"No time like the present to learn." He brought his mouth down on mine again.

This time I put everything I had into it. I must've been more convincing, though. And how was he to know that it was fear making me tremble, and not his phenomenal skill at love-making?

The problem was, I had been too successful. He was moving me across the room before I realized where he was headed. And even if that strongbox and the canister of poison hadn't been on display there, I had no desire to end up with him on the bed

I was not that good an actress.

CHAPTER THIRTY-FOUR

I planted my feet as firmly as I dared without seeming that I was going to wrestle him and said, "Speaking of Mary, I think her idea had some merit. Don't you think it would be appropriate if we had a drink before...before we continue?"

"Before lunch?" his eyebrows went upward. "I didn't remember you as being much of a drinker."

"It is an occasion, isn't it?" I said with what I hoped was a giddy laugh. "I was thinking of something festive. Some champagne, even. Do you suppose there's any in the house?"

I wondered if I ought to emphasize that I was nervous over what was going to happen. But on second thought, I might have quite a bit more time to get through, and I didn't want to sound convinced that anything was going to happen.

He seemed altogether willing to go along with whatever I desired, however. "I think there's champagne down in the cellar," he said with that same air of amused tolerance. The man must be all ego.

"Darling, can we?" I fluttered and smiled and looked with no effort whatsoever tremulous.

"Of course."

I had to suppress a big sigh of relief when we were out in the hall and going downstairs. If I could only continue stalling until I could somehow make a break....

I got my first real spark of hope when we got to the cellar door. There was a big old key in the lock, the old fashioned sort of lock. If I could persuade him to go down to the cellar without me, just long enough for me to close the door and turn the key....

He wasn't having any of that, however.

"You go ahead," I said, holding back in the kitchen. "I'm not much for creepy cellars and old spider webs."

He opened the door and put out his hand for mine. "Nothing to be afraid of here. I guarantee nothing but the best spider webs. Besides I'll hold your hand. I might even kiss you."

I couldn't, since I was supposed to have fallen head over heels again, refuse that offer. "A girl would be crazy to pass up an invitation like that." I gave him an overwhelmed look.

I took his hand and we started down the steep stairs. "But if one spider makes a face at me, you'll have to carry my body back up."

He didn't laugh, and after the words were out of my mouth, I didn't find them particularly funny, either. It came to me then that maybe I wasn't being so clever as I had thought. For all I knew, this was where he had planned to do it anyway. There might already be a shallow grave dug down here.

We were halfway down when the lights went out.

"Easy," he said, squeezing my hand. I must have jumped a foot and a half. I know I squealed. I had intended to scream, but a squeal was all that came out.

"It's just the storm. I'm surprised those lines haven't gone before this. I'll go back up to the kitchen and get the torch. You stand right there and don't try to move."

"I couldn't, my legs are paralyzed."

They remained that way until he'd almost reached the dim rectangle of light from the kitchen door when I remembered the key in the lock and what I had been planning to do to him.

"Oh," I gasped and bolted upward, almost knocking him over.

"Hey." His arm came about my waist. I was shaking like a leaf. "Something wrong?"

"Only...I thought I heard something move down there. I'm scared to death of the dark."

"We could let the celebration go until afterward." He gave

my waist a squeeze.

I had too good an idea, however, of what he meant by afterward. "No, it's all right. I'm just afraid of being alone in the dark. Let's get the torch. Besides I'm not going to be cheated out of a real toast. I had in mind throwing the glasses into the fireplace."

"In that case," he said, leading me the rest of the way into the kitchen, "we better not use the good Baccarat. Mary would really give me the devil over that."

How could she, I ask myself silently, if we were on our way to London?

He found the torch and we started back down again. I was sorry now that I had played it like such a scardey-cat. I had to go on clinging to him, which gave me little opportunity to escape.

He found the champagne all too quickly. Someone had placed it right smack on the first shelf he went to. He held the bottle up to the light. He had let me go however, to manage that. I took a step back away from him and pretended to be peering at the shelves.

"That's the white stuff, isn't it?" I asked with all that ignorance I could put into my voice.

He chuckled and said in his best school master's voice, "Champagne is all white, darling."

"Oh no. I had some one time with a friend, and it was red, like regular wine. I was rather hoping that was what you'd have."

"Sparkling burgundy?"

"Was that it? Just like champagne, only red."

"Must've been. My dear, you do have common tastes, don't you?"

How I'd like to have retorted to that. But he was looking along the shelves, as I had hoped he would, and this was no time to go salving my ego.

I pulled a bottle from the shelf nearest me and examined the label. "Would this be it? It says Graves."

"Then it is probably Graves, my pet," he said, turning away for me.

"And it wouldn't do?"

"A little heavy." He moved away a few steps.

No, I thought, just about heavy enough.

The torch light threw the perspective off, though. It did not hit him squarely, as I had intended, but slid off the side of his head. He staggered, falling forward and putting out a hand to brace himself against the shelves. I saw the shelf sway. I grabbed, praying that it was not attached to the wall. It fell with him and across him, bottles crashing and shattering all about.

I didn't wait to see if he was still conscious. The light had gone out but glow from above guided me in the right direction. I felt with my hands, stumbling as I did on a rolling bottle. I found the hand railing and scrambled upward.

Below me, more bottles crashed and banged as he tried to dig out from the debris heaped upon him.

"Damn you," he swore, "I'll...."

I never did hear what was he was going to do. I slammed the door shut on the rest of his oath and gave the key a turn.

For a moment I stood leaning against the door, trying to catch my breath. My legs were suddenly all weak, and I reminded myself that I was still recovering from arsenic poisoning.

I heard him bounding up the steps. I whirled and backed away from the door. In terror, I thought, what if the lock doesn't hold?

It did. He rattled the knob and banged on the door, shouting, "Chris, what on earth is this all about? Let me out of here, for god's sake."

Not on your life, I thought. I turned and ran from the kitchen.... And stopped dead in my tracks.

I suddenly understood why Jeff had not made an issue of the open strongbox on the bed. Why, although he had probably seen it, he had gone along with my silly little game. No wonder he had been amused and in no hurry.

There was, after all, nowhere for me to go. The storm outside had me trapped here, just as Jeff was trapped in a cellar.

CHAPTER THIRTY-FIVE

I stood for a moment in stunned silence, my mind whirling like the gusts of snow outside. I had seen the storm beyond the windows, violent and threatening. The servants, all local people, had left long ago, realizing that they would otherwise be trapped here. Phone lines and power lines were down.

So I needn't entertain any thoughts that Jeff had exaggerated that part of it. The storm had merely worked out well in his favor, although I felt certain without it he would have found some other way of keeping me here until he was ready to spring his trap.

From behind me I heard him pounding on the cellar door again. Would it hold him, and for how long? The pounding had stopped and I could imagine Jeff on the other side of that wooden barrier, his mind already at work.

He would not have to range far afield to find a way out of the cellar. There were windows. They were high up and small, but I had no doubt that he could escape by one of them. And even if I locked the doors of the house, he could enter it in like manner.

Knowing Jeff, I felt certain that not even the possibility of getting caught would deter him now from seeking me out and finishing what he had started. I must have dealt an awful blow to his ego. No, I was not safe here merely because Jeff was locked for a few minutes in the cellar. The storm outside the house was no more threatening than the one that had been engulfing me within. I had only one hope, however slim of saving my life, and that was by escaping.

It took only seconds to race up to my room to find my warmest clothes and put them on. Yet, it seemed an eternity. I put on double pairs of stockings and my old walking shoes. My own slacks seemed too thin but I found a pair of thick corduroy pants in Jeff's room. They had to be rolled up and there was room enough in them for a good-sized papoose, but they were warm. Sweaters, my knitted scarf, gloves. My coat was downstairs. I was ready.

In the hall I came to a stop again. Mary was still here, unconscious in a drunken stupor. Dare I leave her with Jeff?

I thought so. He was a cunning man. He might, enraged and his vanity wounded, kill me blindly, but his instinct for self-preservation would protect Mary.

I was about to open the door from the kitchen to the outside when I heard faintly the sound of breaking glass coming from the cellar.

I flattened myself against the kitchen door and thought frantically. The cellar windows were all to the rear. He must be climbing out that way. In a moment he would be outside, then he would come to this door or these windows. I would have to escape from the front.

I ran down the long hall to the front door, praying that in his anger he would take the most obvious route, and not try to outwit me.

I threw open the front door and ran out into the storm raging outside.

It was like moving through a swirling fog of white flakes. It might have been night, so little light penetrated the snow. The wind fought against me savagely, trying to push me back, as if it resented my intrusion into its domain.

I fought my way laboriously about the house, trying to avoid putting myself in a direct line with the windows. Not, I reflected grimly, that he would be able to see me if he were inside now. The storm made everything invisible more than a few feet away.

Nothing was familiar in this blinding whiteness. There were no trees where I felt certain there ought to be trees. The terraces where the flowers bloomed in spring had melted away into the white landscape.

The garages were no good to me. I didn't know how to drive the car, and anyway I didn't think I could find the road. I went directly for the stables. The animals there were familiar with the terrain. Trust a horse to find his way

What I had foolishly not anticipated was that the stables would be locked. Of course the man who took care of them had gone home with the other servants.

I stood leaning weakly against the rough wood of the door, wishing I could remember the building more clearly. Were there windows? I couldn't think The wind buffeted me. The snow blinded me. My thoughts would not sort themselves into orderly patterns.

No, no windows, I was sure of it. I took hold of the hasp with its solemn looking lock and rattled it in frustration. Somewhere in the house was a key. Dared I go into the house to look for the key?

It would be near the rear door presumably. In the kitchen. I remembered dimly—or was I only imagining it because I was already cold and exhausted?—Sets of keys that hung near the cellar door.

Where would Jeff be now? Searching the house? His first thought would be that I had hidden myself somewhere. He would go from room to room, checking closets, under beds....

I had left the front door open!

My knees threatened to buckle under me. He knew by now I had fled the house. What destination would be more obvious than the stables? At any moment he would appear through the curtain of snow surrounding me, would reach out to grasp me.

Something slapped against me. I screamed, twirling about, almost falling. It was a piece of canvas torn from its moorings somewhere. It clung to me for a moment, then the wind ripped it loose and it disappeared into the storm.

The Evans house was not far. From what Peter had told me, it was just over a couple of hills beyond the skating pond. But there was another house that was nearer. I had seen it in the distance from a high path. I had never thought to ask who lived there. I had not guessed of them that I would need their help, that my life might depend upon them.

Whoever it was, though, I knew they could not refuse to take someone in from out of the storm. And even if Jeff followed me there, he could not harm me in front of a local farm family. If, I thought grimly I made it that far.

I must, I told myself firmly. But the resolution echoed hollow through my mind as I pushed away from the stables and began to walk, stumbling every few feet.

It was impossible to make anything out even a few inches before me. Shadows loomed up out of the whiteness. I thought the first one was Jeff and barely suppressed another scream. But it was a tree. After that, I decided I was going to need all of my breath for the walk ahead of me.

I went right through some rosebushes, grateful for the heavy pants I had donned. I walked into a fence that ought to have been yards away from me. Some of the snow drifts were hip high already.

It was a walking nightmare. The weight of my clothes dragged me down, the snow and the howling wind tried to hold me back. I stumbled over something buried in the snow and went tumbling into the icy drifts. I struggled to my feet again, thinking that if I only remained in one spot for a few minutes, I would be completely buried from sight.

By the time I reached the edge of the woods I felt as if I had walked halfway around the world. Exhaustion from the arsenic poisoning fought against the strength that fear gave me. I dared not think of the outcome of the combat.

Impossible to try to follow the path, long since buried in the snow. I would have to trust to instinct to carry me in the right direction, skirting the thickest part of the woods and climbing uphill. Then I must cut directly across the hills.

My feet and hands were numb already. My nose, under the knitted scarf, was a piece of ice. I came to another fence that I did not even remember. I fell over rather than climbed it.

In the woods, even the thinner portions of the edges, it was a bit easier. The trees offered some break from the wind, and the snow was not quite so deep. I must have veered from the path, for I found one of Peters traps, set I knew not how long ago, with a rabbit in it. The poor creature was frozen solid.

I could no longer guess if I were going in the right direction. Every tree looked alike, and about them all hung the white sheets of snow. I prayed to whatever guardian angel had protected me so far that I might not be walking in a big circle, right back into Jeff's waiting arms.

Somehow I was going right, though. I came to a thicket that I thought I recognized.

Just beyond it I fell again.

I lay for a moment on the frozen ground, the snow already hurrying to throw its protective shawl across me. I can't go on, I thought.

From somewhere in my frightened mind came a vision of David whispering, "I love you."

I scrambled to my feet again. I must think of David, only of David. Think of happy things. My apartment in New York. Peter Evans' laughing face. David, holding me....

Memories ran together, blurring as the landscape was blurred before my eyes. I shook my head and pushed on, not daring to pause for breath, although my chest was aching. The swirling masses of snow were a sea of whispering voices, warning me that I would never make it, reminding me of how cold and tired I was.

I had gone wrong after all. I had come to the stream below the pond. It was wide here and deep.

I hesitated. To avoid it I would have to climb the steepest part of the hills. If I crossed here, the ground was easier climbing.

"If the ice breaks, they won't find me tell the spring thaws," I told myself aloud. I put one foot cautiously on the ice. It creaked but it held.

I moved slowly, pausing at each step. Once I fell down, and

my heart stopped in that instant before I hit the ice. If ever I went through, I would never escape the icy water.

It held. It was a moment before I could summon the courage to go on. I did not even try to stand and walk but remained on hands and knees, crawling. I actually welcomed the frozen ground and clinging drifts of snow on the opposite side.

The ground here sloped upward. I thought I knew about where I was in relation to the farmhouse I was seeking. I went up, the wind at the top of the rise nearly hurling me back down to the stream. I was in the open here, and every step was a test of my strength, the wind thrusting cruelly against me. I clutched my coat tightly about me, bending into the wind, and struggled on.

It had to be here, over this second hill. I peered ahead into the dimness, looking for an outline, a gleam of light, anything that would tell me I had found it.

I almost missed it after all. It lay in a little hollow. I would have gone past it had I not tripped again, tumbling in the snow. My foot was caught, and when I went to free it, I saw that it was entangled in a piece of fencing. The low decorative sort used to surround flower beds.

A few steps further on, I found the house, its great shape suddenly hovering before me. I had begun to cry with relief, gasping and sobbing, somehow finding the strength, although my limbs felt literally as if they were falling off, to stagger to the house.

I leaned against the rough walls. It was dark, but the power was off, and probably the people within had been found without candles or lanterns. It didn't matter. There was surely some sort of heat within, and it was at least shelter from this awful world turned white and gray.

"Hello," I called aloud, not sure I could make it the rest of the way. If only they would come for me. If only David were here to pick me up in his powerful arms, as he had done before, to carry me to safety....

I had nearly blacked out. My senses came back as I sank to

my knees in the snow. Bitter, I thought, to die here, inches from safety.

No, something within me cried silently. Holding to the wall, I got up again. My hand guided me along the wall. I had a moment of joy as I felt the window sill. I lifted my hand to pound on the window—and put it through the open space that ought to have been filled with glass.

I had come to a deserted shell of a house.

CHAPTER THIRTY-SIX

Never in my life had I felt so defeated, so ready to give it all up, as I was in that awful moment of realization. The house was deserted, its windows broken out. There was no one to answer my cries, no waiting warmth of the fire, no help from pursuing horrors.

"You must go inside," I told myself aloud, speaking as I would to some wayward child. I willed my feet to move, my mind to be still. All was not yet lost. Fire or no fire, inhabitants or no inhabitants, the house offered shelter from the storm. Perhaps I could build my own fire. At the very least, I would be out of this wind and snow.

Not entirely, of course. The wind whipped through the broken windows and open doors and there were drifts of snow on the floors and in the corners. But in contrast to what I had gone through the last hour or so—I have no idea how long I really had been out in the storm—it was a veritable isle of comfort.

I had no matches with which to start a fire. It was the only time in my life I envied those smoking girls. A good girl scout would presumably have been able to start a fire without matches, but I have often had trouble getting the gas range in my apartment to light properly.

All I could do was find the most protected spot in one of the rearward rooms, huddle into the corner, and pray for the storm to end.

At least I could get my breath back, feel a little of the strength returning to my weary body. I wished I had thought to bring some food. I would have welcomed almost any kind of nourishment now, even some arsenic-saturated stew.

Better not start thinking about food, I warned myself. nor how cold you are.

I shrank down into my coat as best I could, leaving nothing uncovered but my eyes, and those I closed.

I might have dozed. It seemed as if time had passed without my awareness of it. I opened my eyes, staring straight ahead without blinking.

Some sound—only the shack creaking in the wind? Or was it a new sound? When I heard him stumble against the half open front door with a whispered oath, I knew only too well that it was not the shack creaking. Jeff had followed me here.

Perhaps he had guessed rightly that this being the closest shelter, it was where I would head. Or perhaps, close on my heels, he had gotten some glimpse of me. I cursed myself silently, realizing for the first time that I was wearing my bright red coat, like a signal flare for anyone pursuing me.

He was at the front door. There were four rooms to the house, and I was in the rear one. No hope of trying to hide myself in an empty shell. There was only one thing I could do.

I crawled out the open window into the storm again, dropping noiselessly into a deep bank of snow.

And now, I thought, getting dazedly to my feet, I must pray.

And pray I did, staggering blindly through the still raging blizzard. I went in the direction of the Evans home, although I knew I hadn't a chance of making it that far.

I exhausted my strength and went on, my feet moving of their own accord, lifting, falling, lifting, falling, carrying me laboriously forward. I was beyond fear even, too weak for that powerful emotion.

I reached the edge of the wood, circling about and above it, in the direction of the pond. The path through the woods would be easier but much longer. Better to stumble over this crest, onto the next.

The wind changed.. It seemed to be calling my name. "Chris!"

it cried on an ascending scale. "Chris, wait!"

The last of my hope gave out. That was no ghost-call of the wind, but a human voice. Jeff's voice, calling after me.

He was still in pursuit. Close enough to see me and my red coat.

I struggled out of the coat as I ran clumsily onward. My fingers could barely manage the buttons and I ripped them loose. I threw the coat aside, the wind rushing to embrace my sweater clad body.

I was colder, I suppose, but the point was really moot, since I already felt frozen. I could hope that he might not be able to follow me as easily. And I could run faster without the added weight. Not a great deal faster, because my feet weighed a few tons each and were getting heavier with each step.

Almost to the pond. How far had Peter said beyond it? A half-mile? Impossible to make it, and yet I must try, must go on, stumbling, staggering, falling....

I could not get up again. I was at the bluff over the pond, at the very spot from which he had shot at me. I thought of the pond, of flying free across the ice, with the surface like crystal and the sky blue and a snowbird swooped and calling overhead. The lingering scent of dead leaves and withered growth.

I could go no further. I hadn't the strength to rise again. My lungs felt ready to burst, my heart banged violently against my ribs.

I looked back the way I had come. For a second or so there was nothing but the swirling whiteness. Then a shadow appeared, growing larger and darker, becoming the shape of a man.

He looked only slightly less exhausted than I. He staggered up to me, stumbled, and literally fell across me. His breath came and went with a rasping croak.

I saw his face and knew that it was not physical strength alone that had enabled him to pursue me over this torturous snow driven path. His face was twisted with hate and loathing and a fury as violent as the winds howling about us. His lips were blue, his eyebrows covered with frost. He looked like some awful creature from the ice age, a nightmare horror from some Hollywood movie.

"You....," he gasped, getting to his knees. "Damn you, damn you, damn you!"

I tried to speak, to say something, anything to ease the horror that I saw in his eyes, but I hadn't even the breath left for that. No words came, although my frozen lips were moving.

"I...I'm going to...to kill you," he rasped.

His hands, like blocks of ice, found my throat. His eyes locked on mine as his fingers tightened, cutting off my labored breathing.

Dear god in heaven, I thought as the ground began to sway beneath me, only a miracle could save me now.

CHAPTER THIRTY-SEVEN

I got my miracle, a childish miracle fashioned from the ice and snow and frost, with a sparkle of winter sunlight for hair.

"Miss Chris."

The wind again, I thought. The wind, calling my name. But I can't come and play, not today.

The fingers tightened, tightened.

"Stop it, let her go."

The hands were gone from my throat and I fell back to the ground. Jeff clambered to his feet, flailing out at something. I had a vision of white skin and golden hair.

It was Peter, ducking Jeff's clumsy blows, trying to get to me where I lay in the snow. Something fell, one of his traps that had been draped over his shoulder.

Struggling to get air into my tortured lungs, I got to my knees. I could get no further. Crouched like some animal, I watched my young snow-image battle for my life.

It was grotesque, the combat in the snow. Peter was young and lithe and for all his years, strong. Jeff had a man's strength but it had been sapped by weeks of illness and by the horrible chase through the snow.

Peter's foot slipped in the snow. Jeff lunged. Desperation gave him a strength he might otherwise not have possessed. I saw Peter struggling to free himself from that awful grip, hands waving furiously.

He must have realized himself that he might not escape, because he suddenly yelled, "Run, Chris. Run."

I tried, too. Somehow, from some final source within I found the strength to get to my feet, swaying in the blast of the wind.

Peter had broken loose. He stumbled again, scrambling toward me.

Jeff had other advantages in a fight such as this, he knew no scruples and he now had nothing to lose. Like the fox in the story, he was in for a hen, he might as well be in for the flock.

"Peter," I cried, or rather tried to cry, for it came out no more than a squeak.

I saw Jeff stoop, I saw the trap in his hand, held by its chain. He swung it like a sling. The cruel metal caught Peter on the crown of his head. He gave a cry of pain and toppled to the ground.

Jeff turned to me again. The force of his anger was like a blow that made me step back even as he swung the trap again, at me!

It cut the air a fraction of an inch in front of my nose, whistling past me.

He was on the verge of exhaustion, though and the force of that swing, its momentum when I failed to stop it, threw him off balance.

He turned with the swing of it, swaying to the side, stumbling. His foot went out to the side and came down on the snow covered edge of the bluff.

He went without a cry. Perhaps his strength, too was gone. One moment he was there before me. The next he was rolling and tumbling down the steep fall, sending clouds of snow into the air, until he had disappeared from sight in the storm. I thought I heard him land with a crash below, but it may only have been my imagination, a trick of my tortured brain.

* * * * * * *

I thought we were done for anyway, I too weak to stand, Peter struck unconscious, perhaps already dead.

I went to where he was lying in the snow, but he was only

stunned, and even as I fell to my knees beside him, he moaned and stirred.

In a moment he opened his eyes and would have jumped to his feet, but I put a hand out to touch his cheek.

"It's all right," I said, "he's gone."

He smiled, a young man's smile, as bright and as unconcerned as if we had just met for skating on the pond, as if a moment before we hadn't been engaged in a life and death struggle.

That was the last I remember, his smile, dazzling in all that snow. I had a sensation of drifting, being carried by a gust of wind, into darkness.

* * * * * * *

It wasn't the wind that carried me on that fateful day—it was David.

"When I had time to cool off," he explained, "I realized what a lout I had been and tried to call. As soon as I learned about the storm and that the house was cut off like that I rushed back. I had a devil of a time getting there at all, but I had taken the Land Rover—they'll go through anything. And when I found you and Jeff both gone and the house wide open, I knew things had really gone bad. I had just arrived at the Evans' house to try to get together a search party when Peter came stumbling in."

We were at Morgan House, in the sitting room. It was several days since our tragic scene in the snow, and it was nearly time to go to the train station, to catch my train back to New York City.

"Peter was the real hero, of course," David said.

"I didn't really suspect anything about Mr. Linton," Peter said, embarrassed and pleased all of the same time. "But when my grandma came home and I heard everybody had left you there, and I remembered you had been sick, I thought somebody ought to look in on you. Plus, you had talked like you might be in some kind of trouble. So I made up an excuse about having to check my traps and talked my dad into letting me go out. I was on my way here when I saw the two of you on the bluff."

"And none too soon either," I added, "my little hero."

"I didn't really do anything," he disclaimed modestly, blushing, but with a proud gleam in his eyes.

"Didn't do anything?" I lifted an eyebrow. "No, you only braved a blizzard that would have scared any sensible adult, and then took on a murderous man, afterward carrying me nearly all the way to your home. Darling boy, I owe you my neck for whatever it's worth, many times over."

Peter had managed to carry me most of the way home, and when he couldn't carry me further, he'd left me in the shelter of a tree and run the rest of the way to get help, arriving just before David.

"We both owe you a great deal," David said, putting an arm around me. "I only wish I'd been there when I was most needed."

"You mustn't blame yourself. It was I, after all, who drove you away. I owe you every kind of apology for not being able to believe in us. I should have. If I had, none of that would have happened. And Jeff...."

"Jeff was dead when we found him," David said. "I think he may have broken his neck in the fall, but anyway he wouldn't have survived long in the snow."

"A fate I nearly shared," I said, shaking my head with the memory.

Mary Linton came in just then. She was too well bred to let all of what she must have suffered show. She still looked proud and imperious and utterly elegant. But she had aged frightfully in a matter of days, and one could see, in the faint trembling of her hands, in the inability of her eyes to remain on you for long, that it cost her dearly to have to face us just now, especially me.

She came to me without flinching, however, and put out a hand as I stood. "You'll be leaving soon," she said, not quite able to meet my eyes. "Before you go, I want to extend my apologies. I'm afraid I behaved very badly."

"With considerable justification," I said, giving her hand a squeeze. "And I'm truly sorry for all you've suffered."

"I think indirectly you saved my life," she said. "And I am

grateful."

But I did not think that she truly was. I think she had loved Jeff deeply, if not wisely. At the moment I did not think life was something she valued very highly.

Mrs. Evans came in to tell me that it was time we were going if we wanted to catch the train. She wished me well also.

"Will you be coming back?" Peter asked at the door.

It was David who answered. "She'll be back." His arm about my waist tightened gently but firmly.

"Good," Peter said. "You never did get that spin right, you know."

I laughed and hurried down the stairs with David. The ground was still white with snow, but it glistened now in bright sunlight that turned the whole world to crystal.

The storm was over.

ABOUT THE AUTHOR

V. J. BANIS is the critically acclaimed author ("the master's touch in storytelling..."—*Publishers Weekly*) of more than 200 published books and numerous short stories in a career spanning nearly a half century. A native of Ohio and a longtime Californian, he lives and writes now in West Virginia's beautiful Blue Ridge.

You can visit him at http://www.vjbanis.com